Killing Time
In Taos

a mystery by

J. Timothy Hunt

ADHEMAR PRESS

TORONTO

Adhemar Press
Toronto, Ontario
Canada

Visit us on the World Wide Web:
http://www.adhemarpress.com
or email us at:
editor@adhemarpress.com

National Library of Canada Cataloguing in Publication

Hunt, J. Timothy, 1959-
Killing Time in Taos
ISBN: 0987804405
ISBN-13: 978-0-9878044-0-2

J. TIMOTHY HUNT

CHAPTER ONE

Brandon Bennington sat in front of the ruins of the San Geronimo Mission with the end of his number 2B pencil clenched firmly in his teeth. In the open sketchbook on his lap he had drawn only a crude outline of the church bell in the tower and a few scratchy indications of the melted remains of two thick adobe walls. In truth, Brandon wasn't looking at the mission at all. His attention was drawn elsewhere, across the wide dirt plaza of the Taos Pueblo that was scattered about with shiny new rental cars, scruffy packs of mongrel dogs and camcorder cowboys. He was watching his neighbor, Ethan Arnold, taking pictures without his shirt on.

Ethan was a photographer staying two doors down at the same artist colony. Brandon gazed at Ethan as he stood in the afternoon sunlight with his shirt tied casually around his waist, absorbed in setting f-stops and twiddling knobs.

In the two weeks since Brandon's arrival in New Mexico, Brandon and Ethan had developed nothing more than a nodding acquaintance. They had never spoken, had never introduced. Brandon wondered if Ethan even knew his name.

Probably not, he thought. As Brandon continued peering at Ethan over the top of his drawing pad, he instinctively began cataloguing Ethan's parts, noting the play of light off his freckled trapezius and deltoid muscles, the strong arch of his erector spinae, the strawberry dusting of hair over his pectoralis major, and the two dimples of the gluteal fascia in the small of his back.

Brandon was sitting on a banquette of adobe between a beehive oven and a turquoise blue doorway labeled "Gift Shop." The blue screen door banged open and a small blond child in a plastic cowboy vest came bounding outside, beating on a toy tom-tom, shouting "Woo woo woo!" The boy tripped over Brandon's extended legs and landed face down in the dirt sending his little toy drum rolling out onto the plaza. There was an obligatory moment of stunned toddler silence before some fierce wailing began and the boy's mother appeared to dispassionately hoist her son up and dust him off.

Amid the ever increasing squall from the child, Brandon got up and handed the little boy back his drum. When he glanced up again, he saw Ethan looking directly at them, smiling and nodding. Brandon nodded and grinned shyly back. Suddenly, he felt an intense need to sit back down and concentrate wholeheartedly on his drawing of the mission.

Out of the corner of his eye, he saw Ethan once again fiddling with his camera. Now he was taking Brandon's picture. Being reticent to look back up, Brandon decided to act like he didn't notice. Immediately, however, he felt ridiculous as he tried not to model, yet at the same time, tried to look photogenic.

After what felt like an eternity, he finally heard the crunch of sneakers approaching. From out of his bowed perspective, Brandon caught a glimpse of Ethan's feet. He looked up with an expression he hoped would approximate pleasant surprise, and waited for Ethan to say hello.

"Hello," said Ethan.

Silence. The ball was now in Brandon's court.

"Hi," he rejoined. More silence. "It's pretty hot out here, isn't it? The light's good, though. For taking pictures and stuff. I mean, it's good for me, too, for drawing 'cause it makes shadows. Anyway. The Indians make you pay twenty bucks to draw or paint here. Oh, I see you had to get one of those things, too. A permit. Probably cost you about the same, I guess. They probably make a lot of money off the tourists taking pictures – not that you're like a tourist. I mean you've got a camera, but … well, you know."

Ethan looked at the yellow photo permit dangling from a string on his camera strap, then looked back down at Brandon. He grinned. Brandon grinned also and looked away. A swarm of gnats in the distance suddenly became very interesting.

"I'm going to head back. Want to join me?"

Brandon nodded and gathered his belongings. As they started to walk away together, he decided to contribute one final piece of information. "My name's Brandon."

"I know."

Neither one having a car, the two men began walking the five miles back to the Pembroke Artist Colony which was just to the west of Taos in a section called Cañon. With a few well-placed questions, Brandon found that although normally taciturn, Ethan was in fact quite easy to talk to. It wasn't long before he learned that Ethan grew up in Montana, worked awhile for newspapers in both Austin and New York City, and occasionally wrote books and articles on the photographer Ansel Adams.

As they conversed and plodded along, Brandon kept trying to keep his chin down to shield his brow from sunburning. He originally thought he would fit in fine in Taos because, like the local Indians and Hispanics, he had a thick head of limp, black hair. Unfortunately, unlike the locals, Brandon was unusually skinny, tall, and painfully Caucasian. His skin had a naturally blue-white hue that was becoming more patriotic the longer he stayed in the sun.

A couple of miles went by and they came to an open stretch of road bounded on either side by intermittent strings of rusted barbed wire. There were no buildings or trees in sight, nothing but the gray blue hump of Taos Mountain on their left, miles of pungent sagebrush on their right, and occasional dust devils spinning into the mirage on the distant pavement before them.

As Ethan continued to regale him with the lesser-known facts of Ansel Adams's life, Brandon started to shift his attention from the sunburn on his forehead to the one he was rapidly developing on the back of his neck. He tried placing his drawing pad like a hat on top of his head for a while, but all it did was make the blood rush out of his upheld arms. Ethan looked at him with some concern and said, "Are you going to be all right?"

"No. How much longer do we have to walk? I took a taxi to get out there. It seemed like a long way."

"It's a little more than an hour walk. You should have brought a hat."

"I hadn't planned on walking back. I think my neck's starting to blister."

"Here," said Ethan as he stopped and took the denim shirt from his own waist and tied it around Brandon's head.

Brandon's shoulders unexpectedly stiffened at Ethan's touch. Ethan was close enough for Brandon to smell. Close enough to feel the heat radiating off of his bare shoulders. Brandon's skinny chest started thumping from the adrenaline percolating through his veins.

Ethan smiled.

"What?" asked Brandon.

"You look like Yassir Arafat," he said, "after shopping at The GAP."

Brandon shyly smiled as Ethan looked directly into his eyes. Ethan's blue eyes were flecked with grey, creased at the corners. They absorbed Brandon, becalmed him. Brandon wanted to reach out and do something, say something, but doing nothing, saying nothing, was an enormous task in itself.

It was only for a few seconds that they stood toe to toe, watching each other, until Brandon self-consciously broke away. Mind racing, wondering what might happen next, Brandon let his eyes lower and looked absently at the ditch on the side of the road. Immediately, he caught sight of something bright red in the sagebrush. A shoe. Two shoes and a ... The shock of recognition made him blanch.

Ethan looked puzzled, then also turned his gaze to the right. His eyes focused on the roadside, then opened wide in slow motion disbelief. "Jesus Christ," he said.

In the underbrush of the ditch a few feet away lay a dead human body.

"Don't look," Brandon commanded. He placed a hand on Ethan's shoulder and tried to gently swivel his attention away from the corpse. Ethan, however, was not to be shielded and shrugged off Brandon's mild restraint. He moved toward the body to take a better look. Brandon could do nothing but follow along.

It was the body of a woman. From the state of decay, Brandon quickly assessed she must have been there at least two weeks, maybe more. The lack of rain and the parched high desert air had mummified her, keeping her body from putrefying. Brandon hated it when corpses putrefied. At home in Philadelphia, his job at the medical school was normally unpleasant enough without the smell and the mess. The woman on the side of the road, however, was fairly well intact.

Two large black flies circled over the body's head as it lay face up in the drainage ditch. A wild iris and a small clump of brown-eyed Susans grew up on either side of her. She wore blowzy, cream-colored shorts, a faded red T-shirt and bright red tennis shoes. Across her throat ran a perfectly straight, red-black bruise. Strangled by a belt, Brandon noted to himself, from behind.

Just to confirm his theory, he bent down and lifted the woman's head a bit with a stick to see what he could of the back of her neck. Sure enough, the crossing strap marks left their telltale signature where expected, the ends of the marks trailing upward. The killer was tall then. He was also determined that his victim not be identified. After choking the life out of her, he had taken great pains to hideously disfigure her face, probably with the jagged, bloody rock that lay nearby.

A small movement by his side made Brandon turn and again look at Ethan. Brandon had seen that look before in anatomy class. The glazed stare, the pale greenness that stole over the cheeks. Before he could bark at Ethan to put his head between his legs, Ethan started to melt away in a dead faint. Brandon was only fast enough to grab him by one of the shoulders, but that was enough to slow Ethan's fall and successfully keep him from toppling onto the body. He placed Ethan's head gently on the ground and tried to raise his legs above his heart as he knelt beside him.

As he sat there on the ground waiting for Ethan to revive, Brandon took the time to fully appreciate the peculiarity of his situation. He also took time to notice the insects around him – just as they were taking notice of him. Small red ants and grasshoppers seemed to be everywhere. One of the two black flies left the corpse and buzzed frantically in circles over Ethan's head while other took the opportunity to bite Brandon squarely on the arm.

"Ouch! Damn it!"

Ethan rolled his head lazily to one side and fluttered his eyelids. "What the hell …?" he moaned.

"Hush. Just lie still a moment."

"What happened?"

"You passed out. Don't try to sit up."

Ethan sat up anyway and looked around blankly. All he could see was blue sky, low scrubby plants, and the edge of the old two-lane road that stretched off into the distance. It only took a second before he noticed the woman's body again and it all came back.

Ethan quickly averted his eyes. "Oh God, I'm sorry ... I just ... "

"Don't worry about it," said Brandon soothingly. "This happens around me all the time ... I mean ..." He paused and then continued reluctantly, "in my line of work."

"... your what?"

"I'm an anatomical artist. You know, for a textbook company. I paint stuff, like slices of dead people, for medical books ... you know, and stuff ..." Brandon always kicked himself every time he felt embarrassed about admitting what his profession was, so he decided to end this confession with a statement of dignity and pride. "Basically, I cut up cadavers and paint pictures of them for a living." It didn't have quite the dignified impact he wanted, but at least he tried.

Ethan seemed unfazed by this revelation. To Brandon's great relief, he took this news in stride and started concentrating on what their next move should be. "We have to call the police," he said.

"Where are we going to find a phone?" asked Brandon.

Ethan thought a moment then slowly stood up. "There's got to be one a mile or so up ahead. We're not that far from town. I'll go and get some help and be right back."

Brandon jumped to his feet. "You're going to leave me here?"

"One of us has to stay. It'll make it easier to find this place again."

"I'd rather go with you."

"I run a six minute mile. How fast do you go?"

Brandon paused. "I have to stay here and guard the spot."

Ethan gave him a reassuring pat on the shoulder. "I'll try not to be too long," he said, then turned and started running toward town. Brandon noted that Ethan wasn't lying. He really did run well. Brandon watched with a dazed stare as he receded into the distance.

Once Ethan was out of sight, Brandon turned his attention back to the dead woman. Who was she? Who did this to her? Staring at her, the anatomical artist in him began to surface. He realized that it was rare that he should get a glimpse of a body in such an advanced state of decomposition. The shock of her bashed-in face had worn off, so he opened up his sketchbook, dusted off a clean spot at the pavement's edge, sat down and began to draw.

All the bodies he worked with at the medical school were preserved with formaldehyde. After med students carefully removed the skin, the chemically treated sub-musculature turned shades of reddish brown. Under those circumstances, it was fairly easy for Brandon to forget as he worked that his still life was, in fact, stilled human life. Sitting there in front of a fully dressed specimen, perhaps where she had fallen at the moment of her death, made it much more difficult to regard the dead woman as an inanimate object. It took a few extra minutes before he felt the click in his head that artists feel when they lose themselves in their work.

Brandon enjoyed working in the late afternoon sunlight. Back at his job in Philadelphia, he hated painting under the harsh fluorescent lights of the medical lab, so he frequently took pieces of cadaver home. It was infinitely more comfortable to work at the easel on his balcony. However, his employers frowned on his removal of body parts from the labs, not only because it was against company policy, but mostly because Brandon was not particularly careful. Inevitably he would misplace a bone, or sometimes drop a hand or an ear over the railing. Usually, he would find them days later snagged in the firethorn bushes in front of his apartment building, so Brandon felt strangely at home with dead things tangled in shrubbery.

Completely absorbed in his drawing, Brandon spent the next hour sketching the body and the wild flowers growing at her feet and side. The flow of his composition on the page and the way the iris stole the foreground focus pleased him. If he turned it into a full-scale painting, it would probably be one of his best, albeit unusual, works.

"What are you doing?" said a loud voice.

Brandon jumped a foot in the air in fright. His drawing pad flipped down onto the corpse.

"Jesus, you scared me," Brandon said.

Ethan and a 200-pound police officer stood next to a squad car in the middle of the road. The officer shook his head sadly. "Now look what you did," he said with a soft Spanish accent. "You're messing up the body, man." He walked over and gingerly lifted Brandon's drawing pad from the victim and handed it back to him. "You know, nothing's sacred to you guys, huh? You artist guys, you'll draw anything, won't you?"

Brandon did not quite know what the appropriate response to such a statement should be. He stammered something that sounded like "Well, I, uh," and folded up his drawing pad.

The policeman put his hands on his hips and leaned over to peer at the woman on the road. "Looks like she's been here a long time, huh."

"Looks like it," said Ethan.

"Someone's really took something to her face, too. Yeah. Really smashed it in good. D'you know her?"

"No. Of course not," said Brandon. "We just found her here as we were walking back from the Pueblo."

"Walking, huh?" said the officer.

"Yeah. We're artists staying at the Pembroke Colony. Neither one of us has a car."

The policeman looked at Brandon and Ethan with incredulity then returned his squint to the corpse. "I'd say she's dead," he said and climbed out of the ditch.

His badge read "Benitez #45" and Brandon stood on the roadside and wondered when they started putting an officer's I.Q. next to his name.

From his car radio, Officer Benitez called for assistance in removing a dead body, then took some stakes from the trunk of his car along with a roll of plastic tape emblazoned with the warning "POLICE LINE – DO NOT CROSS." With these, he cordoned off a square area around the body. The fluorescent yellow tape blazed bright as neon in the late afternoon sun. It struck Brandon as ironic that the police would so loudly call attention to a spot they wanted curious onlookers to disregard.

Benitez returned to his car trunk and produced two ice-cold root beers from a cooler. "You wanna pop, Michelangelo?" he offered.

Brandon checked his initial impulse to grab the soft drink greedily and down it in one gulp. He was about to wither from thirst, but he had enough good manners to feign indifference and accept the gift graciously. His mother had taught him well.

His mother!

Brandon had completely forgotten about his mother. Alexandra Bennington Peters was due to arrive in Taos that afternoon at three. By a frantic check of his watch, he realized she had probably been waiting for him at their designated meeting place for two hours. He could picture her parked in a rental car in front of the Chamber of Commerce running the air conditioner until both her hairdo and the Freon went flat.

"I've got to go," he blurted. "I've got to meet my mom."

"Hold it. Where're you going?"

"I have to meet my mother," he repeated. "She's flying in from Washington, D.C. I was supposed to meet her hours ago."

"Well then, she's going to have to wait even longer then, huh."

"Not if I run."

"You're not running nowhere. You gotta stay till the detective arrives and gets your statement."

Brandon was surprised. "Statement?" he said. "What statement?"

"Detective Carson is gonna want you two to stay and give a statement. We gotta have one for our reports."

"We were walking down the road. We found a body. That's my statement. I've got to go."

"You ain't going nowhere, man. Not till Detective Carson gets here."

"Well, where is he? When is he going to be here?"

Benitez gave a fat shrug. "I don't know. They're trying to find him. He was supposed to be in Tres Piedras, but he could be anywhere."

Ethan took a slug of root beer. "Tres Piedras. That's forty miles away."

"What am I supposed to do about my Mom? I can't just leave her sitting in a parking lot all night while you track down some guy."

The officer thought a moment. "I could have someone pick her up," he said.

"Yeah, great idea," Brandon replied sarcastically. "Send a squad car around for her." Then he actually thought about the offer for a moment. "Wait a minute. Are you serious?"

"About what?"

"Could you send a police car out to meet her?"

"Course."

"It'll make my excuse for being late seem a lot more plausible," he said confidentially to Ethan. "Yeah! Have the police pick her up."

The officer shrugged again and said, "If that's what you want, man. We can have someone keep her at the station till you get there."

As he saw the officer reach for the radio handset, Brandon quickly clarified himself, "Wait! I don't want you to detain her or anything. You're not going to do that, are you? I was just wondering if you could send someone around to entertain her for a while."

"You want me to send a police car to entertain your mother?"

"Well … yes," said Brandon. "I mean, my mother probably would find being taken to jail somewhat entertaining, but I don't want her to go there. She's a little … unusual. In fact, she'll probably even insist on being taken to jail if she so much as looks at a policeman for five minutes. She's like that. I know her. She's very curious. She'll probably want to know everything about the policeman's job, including what his jail looks like, but don't actually take her to the jail. For your sake. Just make her dinner reservations, okay?"

The police officer stood still and stared at Brandon with the blankest of expressions. The handset was still in his hand, but he had no idea what to do with it.

"What's the matter?" asked Brandon.

"You want me to call the station and have them send a squad car out to a parking lot to meet your mother – then take her out to dinner?"

"Yes, that would be very nice. Thank you."

Benitez snorted with derision and radioed the police station. After he gave them Brandon's mother's name and description, there was a pause and then a crackly squawk of a reply which Brandon could not understand. The officer asked again for the whereabouts of Detective Carson and the speaker fired back an immediate, and longer, reply. The officer looked amazed and then stared at Brandon with one of those "Well-what-do-you-know" looks. He sighed, signed off, and hung up the mike.

"What'd they say?"

"They said your mother's not at the Chamber of Commerce."

"How would they know?" asked an astonished Brandon.

"'Cause she was just over at the police station looking for you."

"Oh. She was probably trying to find out if I was in an accident or something. What about the Detective?"

"They found him, too. He'll be here in a couple of hours."

"A couple of hours?" he moaned. "Is he still in Tres Piedras?"

"No, he got back," said the officer. "He stopped back at the station house and now he's out to dinner."

"We have to sit here and wait while this guy goes out to dinner? That's ridiculous!" said Brandon. "What am I going to do about my mom?"

"She's being taken care of," replied the officer.

"They're letting her wait at the station?"

"No," said the fat policeman. "She's with Detective Carson at Lupita's Cafe. You better get comfortable. He's a slow eater."

Ethan laughed, then yawned and stretched his arms. Brandon wilted and sat down on the edge of the road, his drawing pad in his lap. The setting sun threw long shadow ribbons from the yellow police tape onto the corpse. Brandon stared at the woman's body anew and, taking up his pad, started to draw her from a fresh perspective. For the first time he noticed that on the rubber edge of each sole someone had written the word MAMA. Brandon thought this was certainly an odd thing to write on one's sneaker, but he recorded it faithfully in his drawing. He also noted that the woman's withered fingers were still adorned with four large rings and her nails still held their opalescent polish.

The policeman popped open another root beer and plopped back down inside his car. Ethan sat on the road next to Brandon. Their knees grazed. Staring at the corpse, Brandon suddenly felt acutely alive.

CHAPTER TWO

"Of course, I didn't believe you'd been killed in a horrible accident, sweetheart, but after two hours of waiting in that parking lot, what would any mother have done? Now really, how could you have faulted me?"

Brandon's mother rolled down the window of the rental car and breathed in the sage-spiced evening air. "And of course, that Detective Carson was lovely. We talked and talked and talked. Related to Kit Carson, you know, but only distantly. You've heard of him, haven't you? Kit Carson? Very famous cowboy or something. Famous. World known, at least so I'm told. Well I knew everything would work out, and see? So it has. But you have to admit, Brandon, it was fortunate I went straight to the police station looking for you, because as it turned out, there were sinister overtones. Imagine, a dead woman being murdered! It was murder, wasn't it? Oh, of course it had to be."

Brandon pulled the car into the drive and then ushered his mother through the front door of his adobe house. She was still talking in a breathless stream of words when suddenly she paused and shot Brandon a frightened look. "You didn't bring her here, did you? The murdered girl?" she asked.

"Well, of course not," said Brandon with surprise. "Why?"

"The room smells like Death," she said.

Brandon felt a quick twinge of panic, then his panic turned to indignity. Not only should his house not smell of dead bodies, his house shouldn't smell of anything at all. The previous night, he scrubbed until the wee hours of the morning anticipating his mother's triumphant arrival.

"Well, Mother," he said with a measured amount of restraint, "if you don't like my house, just say so."

"No, sweetheart," she said, "it's delightful, really it is." She loosened the knot of the dramatic paisley scarf that was draped around her thin shoulders and unwrapped as she toured the room. Brandon saw that she held her scarf tightly clasped in her hands as if to restrain herself from giving everything she saw the white glove treatment. He was annoyed, but grateful.

In preparation for his mother's visit, Brandon had swept up a pound of dirt from the living room floor, and two pounds of dirt from the bedroom. This was not an unusual bit of cleaning for a Taos resident to do. Every home in town had an eight-inch-thick roof of adobe clay which slowly sprinkled down from between the boards on the ceiling like flour through a sifter. Brandon made it a point to sweep all night to ensure that his mother wouldn't be tempted to think he was living in some sort of archaeological dig.

She stopped by a brown and ochre abstract painting by an unknown artist and pretended to admire it. He could tell she was doing her best to look like she approved of his house, but it was obvious to him what she was really thinking. "It's so ... well, it's just so you, but really dear, I'm afraid someone is dead in this room."

"It's clean!"

She paused, closed her eyes and sniffed at the air. "There," she said, pointing to large wooden chest under the window. "There's someone dead in there."

"No one is dead in that box." Brandon replied rather huffily. "I don't smell anything."

"You wouldn't. You have no sense of smell at all, you know. Never have. That is precisely why you can wallow in these so called 'artist colonies' for months on end without turning the slightest shade of green. Really, dearest, I'd suggest you open up that chest … if you dare."

"I can't. I don't have the key," he said, and it was true. The chest by the window served as an end table so there was no reason for his host to provide him with a key. Usually artist colonies furnish their studios with all manner of second-hand furniture – everything from the quaint to the bizarre – and Brandon's new home at the Pembroke Colony of Taos was no exception. The decor was a jumble of rough-hewn south-western artwork tossed together with garish and badly worn upholstered pieces from the 1960s. Brandon liked to think of the effect as a whimsical blend of Connie Francis and Old El Paso.

"Well, you have to open it," she said and started removing the Anasazi souvenir pot and Indian blanket from the top of the chest.

"Mother, you haven't been here for five minutes. Why don't you just sit down for a moment and we'll take care of that later."

"You've got to be joking," she said. "If you've got a screwdriver, we can pry open this lock … no! I have a better idea!" And with that, she pulled two large hairpins out of her thick, blond French Twist, straightened one and bent the other into an odd hook shape. Kneeling before the locked chest, she carefully inserted the pins and slowly worked them back and forth. After several seconds, she snapped open the lock. "There," she said, standing up, "I'm getting out of the way. You open it. I don't want to look inside."

"Where did you learn to do that?" he asked. Brandon had never seen such a thing before.

"What?"

"Where did you learn how to pick a lock?"

17

His mother smiled, re-bent her hairpins and jammed them expertly into her coif. "Your father taught me. In Switzerland." She smiled a knowing smile and said, "It came in handy more than once."

Brandon knew better than to fall into that trap. "Yeah, right," he sighed. "That time you were a Swiss spy." He knew his mother had money, intelligence, and interesting husbands, but unfortunately he also knew she had a gift for fabrication. "Whose safe were you cracking that time?" he asked.

"Never you mind, just open the trunk … carefully," she said and stepped back across the room holding a corner of her scarf over her nose and mouth.

"There is nothing in that trunk," Brandon declared and threw open the lid to prove his point. He did a double take and let out a yelp. Before him lay a dozen furry little mummies – the grisly legacy of a rat family that had lived, loved, and gone to Jesus right there in the box.

"I'll cart this outside," he said sheepishly.

"Do that," she said and opened every window in the house.

Brandon had been very nervous about his mother's arrival in Taos for many reasons, and of course a few of his fears were realized the minute she walked through the door. She never once approved of anywhere he lived during his adult life. Her approval ended with the boarding schools and universities he attended. Of course, the schools were all her idea. She had selected them, inspected them and packed him off to all seven of them herself. Alexandra kept Brandon so mobile during his childhood, it was exceedingly rare that he ever visited his family's townhouse near the nation's capital.

During those years, it was Alexandra's practice to visit her son twice yearly while he was away at school. When he became an adult, she could think of no reason to abandon such a comfortable ritual and continued to jet to his side biannually.

Brandon never looked forward to these visits. Being around his mother for any extended length of time was always unnerving.

Because Alexandra had never been to New Mexico before, Brandon went to great lengths to prevent her from showing up while he was there. Months before his own arrival, he painted dramatic stories about the impoverished conditions in the area. Even though great wealth in Taos was as apparent as great poverty, it didn't stop Brandon from telling his mother that New Mexico was "America's Only Third World State." She came anyway.

The Pembroke Colony of Taos had seven small adobe houses to lodge the artists, like Brandon, who were in residence. The rules there forbade the artists from having phones, televisions, radios, or even mail delivery. The Pembroke Colony was not a place to live comfortably. The Pembroke was a place to work.

The Colony had very strict rules of conduct, which included to Brandon's relief, a no-guest policy. "So you see, Mom," he said, "I'd love to have you stay here, but rules are rules."

"I understand. Now sweetheart, don't worry about me, I'm sure there are lots of lovely inns in and about the area, but really …" His mother got that knowing look Brandon had seen so often and said very conspiratorially, "You know these people don't take the no-guest policy very seriously, don't you?"

"They don't?" he said, "How would you know that? They were pretty good about laying down the law my first day here."

"Then why did they give you a sofa that opens up into a spare bed?"

"It does not," Brandon stated very definitely and walked over to the couch to remove a cushion. Gleaming back at him were the metal mechanism and springs for a hide-a-bed. Brandon became very confused. "Now why would they give me this?"

"So you could have overnight guests, darling," she said. Alexandra proceeded to remove the rest of the cushions and pull the bed out completely. It even had a clean set of sheets on it. "I knew this was a spare bed because convertible sofas sit up a tiny bit higher than plain sofas," she explained. "Besides, I could see a piece of the mechanism sticking out by the back leg. Really, it's just like one your father and I had when we lived in Greece."

"You always told me you lived in Hungary," he said, deciding not to indulge his mother's proclivity for invention.

"We lived in Hungary and Greece. You were born in Athens, you know. It was beautiful." And with that, she stretched out on the sofa mattress and bounced up and down to test the springs. "Go out to the car and get my bags," she said. "Mother is staying."

Brandon knew he couldn't fight her. It was no use pointing out to his mother that he was certainly not born in Greece. It said very plainly on his birth certificate that he was born in Akron, Ohio, but he didn't try to argue with her. Brandon went outside and fetched her suitcases from the car, all the time making a mental note to cancel the reservation he had made at the Taos Inn. For a brief second he even considered using the reservation himself. When Brandon returned to the room, his mother was still bouncing on the bed and singing in a foreign language. She probably wants me to think she's singing in Greek, he thought. He didn't want to get her started, so he ignored her. She's really too much.

Alexandra's view of her own life was a constant problem for Brandon. Ever since he could remember, his mother fancied herself a great authority on many subjects and a traveler of international importance. During her yearly visits, she would chatter on about the places she had seen and the people she had hobnobbed with. (Her most notorious line was, "I just skied with the Pope!") It embarrassed Brandon to think his mother was a chronic liar, but as far as he could determine, there was no basis in fact for any of her stories.

In the middle of Alexandra's second Greek chorus, there was a rap on the back door and Moira Atchison popped her head in the kitchen. "Hello, Brando!" she called out.

"We're in here," he rejoined from the front room and Moira made her entrance. Moira was short and slight with a head that was almost all face. She wore her hair in a sandy, spiky shag that was tucked behind the ears to show off a pair of Christmas poinsettia earrings. Brandon liked Moira immensely because her big, horsey grin always lit up a room. "Hi, Goo, what's new?" he said, "Come in and meet my mom."

Alexandra stayed flat on her back on the bed and lifted a hand to Moira as if she were offering it up for kissing to an Italian Count. "How do you do?" she said.

Brandon rolled his eyes a little and started a polite introduction. "This is my mother, Mrs. Peters. Mom, this is Moira Atchison, better known around here as GooGoo L'Amour."

"So nice to meet you," his mother said and sat up on an elbow. "And I'm better known around here as Mrs. Noble."

Moira looked over at Brandon, who developed a small, pained smile. "What do you mean by that, Mom?" He asked.

"Isn't he just adorable?" Alexandra said to Moira. "Really a fabulous artist, but not a brain in his head. Don't you remember, sweetheart? Mr. Peters passed away. I remarried last spring."

Brandon didn't know what to say. This was news to him, so he just stared with his mouth open. Moira laughed and flopped down next to his mother (whatever her name was) on the mattress.

"You mean Brandon doesn't remember losing his own father, that's terrible!" Moira said with mock shock.

"I'm sure Brandon realizes his own father has passed away, God bless him. Well … God bless them both! His father was a

Bennington – drowned, you know. My last husband was a Peters."

"And he died, too?" asked Moira.

"Yes. Such a tragedy, to be gunned down like that … and at that lovely piazza, too!"

"How awful!" Moira exclaimed and she was just good enough an actress that Brandon didn't know if she were taking his mother seriously or not.

"Yes, it's ruined Italy for me completely, but I'm Mrs. Thornton Noble now. Noble, yes, but not for long. Thornton fortunately survived our wedded bliss, so I'm afraid I'm in the midst of my very first divorce proceeding. A true tragedy. But one has to move on, you know, and I try not to be bitter. So what do you do, GooGoo?" Alexandra asked and laughed at her own sentence.

"She's a playwright," Brandon said, "from Manhattan." The two women glanced over at him for the briefest of seconds.

"Dramatist, raconteur and performance artist," Moira said with much dignity. "Mostly women's pieces, stuff like that, all of them disturbing, all of them brilliant."

"I'm sure they are," his mother said while adjusting her heavy hair. "Would I have seen any of your work in New York?"

"Not unless you have a death wish," Brandon interjected.

Moira gave him a slow look and informed Alexandra that she usually performed at a women's space in the Bowery. "I'm notorious for the rape plays I did there. Violence is my big thing. In my most famous – or rather infamous – piece, I took a raw chicken and ripped it apart on stage, completely covering myself with chicken blood." By the look in Moira's eyes, they could see her envisioning the whole scene. "Then, while I sexually assaulted the carcass, I dropped black balloons on the audience. It sent shivers up their spines. The New York Times loved it."

Brandon's mother didn't even flinch. "I'll wait for the film version," she said.

"All my work is about violence. Violence against women."

"That must be in great counterpoint to the stage name GooGoo L'Amour." Alexandra observed.

Moira laughed. "No! That's just a nickname I got while I've been here. Frank started calling me GooGoo L'Amour to hide the fact he can never remember my name."

"Frank?"

"The Director of the Colony," Brandon explained, "Franklin Crown-Smith. He's this opera impresario who's been running the place for about fifteen years."

"Pompous ass," said Moira. "He scares everyone around here to death."

Alexandra's interest was piqued. "Why is that?" she asked.

"Oh, all the artists around here are a bunch of jerks. Except me and Brandon. They're all afraid he won't like their work. Like anybody really cares what Franklin Crown-Smith thinks, right?"

"I take it, GooGoo, that you don't care," said Alexandra.

"She does, too," Brandon said teasingly.

"I do not!" Moira squealed. "Frank wouldn't know a good piece of performance art if it bit him – and you know, it just might. Or a painting, right Brandon? He burns me up. Frank thinks he's God's Oracle of Art at Taos, but all he knows about is opera. And not even the good operas, either. All he talks about is all these operas that no one's ever heard about."

"Like what?" asked Alexandra.

"Like I don't know, they're so obscure."

Brandon chuckled at Moira and closed one of the front room windows. He explained to his mother that Franklin was supposedly an expert on the operas of Rimsky Korsakov.

"Rimsky-Frigging-Korsakov. Can you believe it?" continued Moira. "Like anyone's ever heard of any operas this guy's written. Can you even name one?"

Alexandra paused and thought for a second. "Well," she said, "there's The Snow Maiden, for one. Didn't he write that, sweetheart?" she asked her son.

Brandon was impressed, but couldn't confirm. Moira, however, was not to be outdone. "Oh, you probably saw it on PBS or something," she said. "And you and Frank were probably the only two people in the world that watched it."

"Perhaps," said Alexandra.

"I was supposed to be on PBS once, but I got bumped for a pledge break."

The pause that followed Moira's last statement clearly called for a change in conversational topic, but Alexandra was eager to hear more about the director of the Colony. "Well, the man sounds perfectly frightful and I'd love to meet him," she said.

"You'll get your chance Wednesday night," said GooGoo L'Moira. "That's what I came over here to tell you, Brando. We're having a big potluck dinner over in Lorna's bungalow and we're asking everyone to bring food and art."

"Food and art," he said, "that sounds dangerous."

"Yeah, it's a noxious compound, but try to be there," Moira replied. "Bring your best painting, a stiff drink and a plate of enchiladas. I'm doing sopaipillas and my tribute to Hedda. It'll be a fabulous evening."

"I can't wait," he sighed. "You think it's okay if Mom comes?"

"I wouldn't want to impose," said his mother, "but I'd love to be there. Especially if you're doing Hedda Gabler."

"No ... Hedda Nussbaum."

"Who?"

"Back in the 'nineties there was a lady in New York whose lover beat her up then killed their adopted kid. I put on a moustache and flog myself. It's brilliant."

Alexandra smiled. "I can't tell if you're joking or not, but it sounds intriguing just the same. Dinner and a murder. I hope they'll let me come."

"Of course it's okay," said Moira to Brandon. "Franklin can pop-quiz her all night about Rimsky-Goddamn-Korsakov. Hey, wait a minute! What about tomorrow night? Aren't you going to take her to Tuesday cocktails?"

Alexandra lit up. "Tuesday cocktails?"

Brandon wrinkled up his nose just like his mother did when she first arrived. "He's not doing it again, is he? I barely recovered from last Tuesday."

"Oh, you gotta go!" said Moira to Alexandra. "Tuesday evenings we all have cocktails at the main house and Franklin plays these scratchy old records for us. Lots of opera and lots of cocktails. If it wasn't for the drinks, the evening would be unbearable. He won't let us talk or anything while the music is playing, like he's trying to educate us or something. Can you believe it? So Brandon and I usually just sit there and get ploughed, right Brandon?"

Brandon flushed. "Well, uh ... not really ploughed, but ..."

Alexandra smiled at Brandon's embarrassment. "Do you know which opera he's planning to play tomorrow?"

Moira screwed up her face and thought. "It's something German this week, I think. He said it's about mythic despair in the modern world. Anyway, he makes the best martini in the state. We have to go."

"I don't want to," said Brandon.

Alexandra got up off the sofa bed and straightened her clothing. Around her in the air was a swirl of fabric and then quickly, her nimble fingers found yet a new way to tie that oversized scarf. "It sounds delightful, Brandon. Of course we'll go; after all, I am the Queen of Mythic Despair. Just think! Opera and cocktails, how civilized ... and right here in America's Only Third-World State! I take back everything I was secretly thinking about your Compound."

"Colony," he corrected.

"Are there any famous artists in residence here, GooGoo?"

"No," said Moira, "Brandon and I are the only ones anywhere near stardom, and we're only on the verge. The rest of the crew are either has-beens or never-wases. Just wait till the potluck and you can decide for yourself. Oh God, Brandon!" Moira turned to him with a horrified expression. "You better drink enough Tuesday to keep you ploughed through Wednesday! Glenda Guilder is going to do a chapter from her latest book on prison reform and that hillbilly kid is going to do a poem. Can you imagine? He's slightly retarded. I don't even think he can read!"

"He must be a good poet," observed Alexandra, "otherwise why would he be here?"

Moira thought deeply about this a moment, then declared, "It's Affirmative Action rearing its ugly little head right here in Taos, New Mexico. So, what did you do today?"

"Who, me?" said Brandon, totally caught off guard. "Well, I uh ... Well, you know, I almost forgot!"

"Forgot what?"

Alexandra sighed and turned to Moira. "Brandon's had a rough afternoon. He walked almost ten miles today."

"Probably fifteen," he corrected.

"Well, you look dead," said Moira.

Brandon and his mother exchanged glances. "I look better than some," he said and reached for his sketchbook. "I was out on the road to the Pueblo this afternoon and found something."

"What? What did you find?" urged Moira, all smiles and anticipation. "Something great?"

"Well, no," Brandon said and opened the sketch book to his second drawing of the dead body. He paused a moment then slowly turned the picture toward her.

Moira at first wrinkled her brow and recoiled a bit from the unexpected shock of what she was seeing. Then her brow relaxed and her eyes grew wide. Continuing to stare transfixed at his rendering of the murder victim, Moira took the sketchbook from his hands and started mumbling over and over, "Oh my God oh my God oh my God ..."

Seeing Moira in such a state, Alexandra quickly intervened. She snatched the sketchbook from Moira's hands, peeked privately at the drawing, then slammed the book shut. "You didn't tell me you drew a picture of it," she said to Brandon. "Is that really what she looked like?"

"I'm afraid so."

"Oh my God!" exclaimed Moira again with mounting conviction. "Is that really a picture of ... of ...?"

"A dead body," said Brandon, a little pleased with himself.

Alexandra, on the other hand, was not pleased one bit. "You should be ashamed of yourself, Brandon! What on earth ever possessed you to show that around to people? How rude! It is a very upsetting drawing, sweetheart. People should not see it."

"I guess I didn't think," he began. "I know it's very graphic, and all but I thought Moira'd like it. I mean, she's the one always going on about women and violence and stuff."

"I hope it didn't upset you too much, GooGoo."

Moira turned on Brandon with an intense, no-nonsense glare and demanded, "Is that really what it looked like?"

"Yes! Yes, that's really really what the dead body looked like! Christ! I'm an artist. I do this for a living and I'm really really good at it. I think I can safely assure both of you that it's an accurate representation of how it looked!"

Brandon's little fit didn't faze Moira. "Did they say who it was?"

"No. No one knows."

"I do," she said.

Alexandra picked the sketchbook back up again to have another peek at the drawing, but even though she was dying of curiosity, she couldn't bring herself to look at it again. "How can you tell?"

Moira took the book from her and opened it back up to the picture. She held it open in front of Brandon and pointed. "Those are my shoes. MAMA's my initials twice in a row. It's what kids used to call me in school. I always write it with a marker on my tennies so I can find them in the pile when I take them off for yoga class. A couple of the other girls I take class with have red shoes, too."

"So who is it?" demanded Brandon.

"Sienna Sandoval. We wondered what happened to her. She just disappeared one day. I lent her some shoes a couple weeks ago after Tuesday cocktails when we had that last big storm and hers got soaked. Oh my God, Sienna's dead!"

Brandon nodded sympathetically. "So she's just some local girl?"

"No!" exclaimed Moira as though he were hopelessly dense. "She was one of the inmates here! A painter. That's the reason you're here, Brandon. She disappeared a few weeks ago, so they gave you her house."

Brandon and Alexandra both stared at Moira, then at each other. Then they stared around the room to make sure Sienna Sandoval was not lurking in the corners.

"You're moving," said Alexandra.

"No, I'm not," said Brandon.

Moira relaxed and shook her head sadly. "I just feel so bad," she said. "Not that she's dead – I mean I'm sad she's dead, too, but – I feel bad that nobody here really liked her very much. That's why nobody really cared when she went away. Except me. And I only cared 'cause she had my shoes." She sighed and tossed his book of drawings aside as if to be through with the whole matter. "I gotta go tell some more people about the potluck. Jesus! Just wait till I tell Lorna what happened to Sienna! She hated her. See you later."

The screen door's tambourine whap punctuated her goodbye.

CHAPTER THREE

By the mirror the next evening, with lipstick poised in hand, Alexandra asked her son, "Just exactly why are you here?"

"You mean here in this room? Or is this an existential thing?"

"Here in New Mexico. I know you're here to paint, but what is so special about this group of little dirt houses?"

"I happen to like these little dirt houses."

"Well, they're charming, I'll grant you that," she said, pausing briefly to blot her lips on a tissue, "but you have no telephone, no television, radio, or mail. You're living just like we did when we were stationed in darkest Africa – and you haven't even left the country! Why would anyone put themselves through this for the sole prospect of free rent?"

"There's a little more to it than free rent," Brandon sighed.

"Like what?" asked his mother.

Brandon was having trouble deciding which shirt to wear to the boring evening of Tuesday Cocktails and was not overly eager to start recounting the Pembroke mystique. It was hard to explain to someone who wasn't an artist why painters for generations have come to Taos. Solitude, of course, is an easy concept to grasp, but to appreciate the rarefied light of the thin, parched, high desert air, it takes a special sensitivity, a special eye. At an elevation of seven thousand feet, the adobe homes, the rugged sandstone boulders – and even mud – in Taos take on a strange glow, as if lighted from within. His mother wouldn't understand this. She would just shrug and say, "Well, it's pretty here, but ..." So he ignored her and selected a blue paisley shirt that he knew she was not fond of.

Alexandra, however, was not to be denied her right of cross-examination. "Brandon," she persisted, "I believe I asked you a question."

"Believe it or not," he said, "this is a very difficult artist colony to get into. Supposedly they only take the very best here, but I have my doubts."

"Doubts about what? The talents of the other people here?"

"No, not the inmates. The warden."

Alexandra continued with her beauty denouement and thought about his accusation. "Franklin Crown-Smith?"

Brandon nodded. "I had to apply to the Pembroke Colony five years before Franklin considered me worthy to come. Every year I'd send him slides of my work and every year I'd always get the same rejection letter. 'My dear Mr. Bennington, although the samples you have submitted show great promise, we do not feel your work reaches the high artistic calibre necessary for residency at The Pembroke. When you have developed a unique and true artistic voice, we look forward to hearing from you again. Sincerely ...' etc."

Alexandra winced and turned the phrase over to herself aloud, "Unique and true artistic voice."

"The gall of it used to raise the hair on my neck," said Brandon. "Still, every year I'd make one more try to prove what a unique and true artistic voice really looked like. I was painting like a man possessed. Wonderful stuff. You haven't seen it yet. I'll show you the slides."

"Please do. But I don't see ..."

"Then I made a mistake," continued Brandon, "and got accepted. Last fall I photographed my latest series of paintings and accidentally ran a roll of film through the camera twice.

Double-exposed every picture. By accident, I sent the botched photos to The Pembroke – and Franklin loved them. So ... go ... figure." Brandon punctuated his last three words by tucking in his shirt in three swift tucks.

Alexandra only lifted an eyebrow in comment over Brandon's chosen attire for the evening, then grabbed her purse and oversized scarf from a chair. "Well, sweetheart, perhaps you stumbled into a whole new artistic arena with those slides. They might have been wonderful."

"No, they were awful," he insisted, "and now that I find out I'm just a last-minute replacement for a woman who was murdered, my estimation of this guy's artistic integrity's pretty low."

"Still, you accepted his invitation," Alexandra noted slyly.

"Well, who wouldn't jump at the chance of free rent?" said Brandon. Grabbing a flashlight from the windowsill, he offered to help his mother on with her wrap before herding her out the door.

It was a chilly high desert evening with a sky ablaze in cold stars. Walking slowly down the long, unpaved driveway that led to the main house, Brandon lit the way for his mother with his rather feeble beam of light. She held tightly to his elbow, stepping carefully over the dried tire track ruts, as all around them night bugs sang in the grass and a light breeze spread rumors from one cottonwood to another.

In silhouette before them was El Casa Grande. As the former summer home of the late catalogue king, Armand Pembroke, the Big House was an organic excess of the local architecture, a sprawling one-story maze of adobe rooms bounded on all sides by lilac hedges and ancient trees. Also, at the end of the driveway, to the right, was a smaller earthen abode known as the Guest House. Armand Pembroke, as far as could be determined, never used the Guest House for guests. Originally it served as the butler and chauffeur's quarters, but now it was just another artist studio at the colony. In fact, Moira was staying there.

At the Casa Grande, Brandon led his mother through a large, carved wood door that opened into a private garden. The little courtyard inside was filled with cacti and flowers dancing in the light of propane torches. They had to pause a moment for Alexandra to make rapturous cooing noises by a terra cotta fountain. Brandon tapped her on the arm and led her gently toward the front door because they were late.

He rang the bell and Crown-Smith's assistant and secretary, PopIris Nelson, answered the door. Iris earned her nickname for her false left eye that was curiously fashioned of solid black glass. Tall and gaunt, with a long neck made even longer by short, blunt-cut hair, she ushered them inside. Trying not to stare at the woman's lost eye, Alexandra gave her best round of warm how-do-you-dos in the dark hallway. PopIris returned these greetings with a small, pained grin and the deadpan gleam of shiny black glass.

"We're a little late," Brandon said. "I hope they haven't started without us."

"No," said PopIris, "you're fine. May I have your coats?"

Alexandra unwrapped herself, looked at PopIris and chuckled.

"Is something wrong?" asked Iris.

"No! I'm sorry. Not at all. Everything is lovely," apologized Alexandra. "Quite impressive. It's just that I keep expecting some strange manservant to pop out of the darkness and ominously say 'Walk this way.'"

Brandon cleared his throat, smiled nervously, and pointed with his thumb off to the left. PopIris nodded and quickly hung their coats up by the door.

"Walk … I mean, follow me," she said flatly.

Alexandra cackled with glee.

PopIris Nelson led them down a long, candle-lit hallway, their footsteps dully thumping on the oxblood floors. Brandon hated walking in the dark, but had to become accustomed to it at the Pembroke. Crown-Smith always insisted that the Casa Grande be illuminated only by fire. It was a romantic notion, but it was also creepy. They rounded a corner then their guide turned to them and unexpectedly smiled as they reached a closed set of dark wooden doors which she swung open dramatically. Brandon's mother gasped in horror and grabbed him by the arm.

The evening gatherings at the Pembroke were always held in the Penitente Room. Brandon forgot to warn his mother in advance of the decor, so Alexandra suffered a bit of a shock.

The Penitente Room was in fact a library that was a re creation of a New Mexican morada, or Penitente church. The only un-churchlike aspect of the library was the south wall bookcase, so large it spanned the entire length of the room, and so tall it required a set of rolling library stairs to access the volumes near the ceiling. The only light in the room came from wax candles in the wooden chandeliers hanging from fierce iron hooks in the ceiling, and from a sprightly fire in the kiva fireplace.

Along the remaining three walls hung a pair of black and brooding Ansel Adams photographs and a series of primitive religious paintings. The paintings were gruesome depictions of Penitente religious rites done in shades of crimson, black and orange. Seen by firelight, the images of torture, self-flagellation and crucifixion were especially unpleasant. Small painted statues of dancing skeletons were dispersed about the scattered pews and tables of the library as were dozens of bloody carvings of Christ on the cross. A huge pot of deep red geraniums on the center table only added to the bloodbath.

Brandon dug his mother's nails out of his biceps and walked her in.

They were the last to arrive. Already present in the room were Moira and Ethan, novelist Glenda Guilder, poet P.J. Copeland, and an unmarried couple from Los Angeles, Lorna Shaw and Brian Epstein. P.J. sat quietly with Ethan, while Moira and Glenda tucked themselves in a far corner of the room deeply engrossed in what appeared to be gossip of profound importance. Brandon waved to try to get Moira's attention, but she didn't notice him.

Lorna and Brian were standing nearby not speaking to one another. Brandon couldn't tell if this was one of those comfortable silences between long-time companions or one of those uncomfortable silences between bickering lovers. Either way, they were the closest people in the room and he wouldn't have to interrupt them to introduce his mother.

"Guys, this is my Mom. Mother, Lorna Shaw and Brian Epstein."

Lorna turned to them and lit up pleasantly as she shook Alexandra's hand. Brian, as incapable of lighting up as a cave at midnight, merely nodded. Alexandra immediately cooed over Lorna's outfit, and indeed Lorna looked particularly dark and ravishing that night. Her long, thick, brown hair cascaded down onto her bare shoulders and the straps of her light summer dress. The dress, made of deep red silk, was a short, sleeveless shift a woman would have worn only as a slip in an earlier era. The silk hugged Lorna's form and displayed her firm, athletic figure as well as the absence of a bra.

Brian was not nearly as well dressed as his girlfriend —or anyone else in the room, for that matter. Jeans, an oversized sweatshirt and his ever present baseball cap was the look he chose for the evening. Alexandra complimented him, too, for looking so "comfortable."

"I'm so excited to be here!" she said. "All you artists banding together in one room ... it's a salon, that's what it is. It's Paris in the 'thirties. All we need is Gertrude Stein and a poodle and it would be perfect, perfect! So what do you do, Lorna? No, let me guess, you look like a great actress ... or an Olympic athlete."

Lorna smiled at the compliment. "I write music," she said. "I'm working on an opera right now. Brian's a sculptor."

"Oh, that's wonderful! Big monumental extravaganzas or do you do wootzie little angels-on-a-pinhead things? The Bible on a grain of rice, you know what I mean ..."

"They're midsized works," said Brian.

"Busts?

"Tombstones."

There was a pause as Alexandra stared at him open-mouthed, then she laughed heartedly at the joke (for she was certain it was a joke) and Brandon could do nothing but laugh along with her, although he felt perfectly foolish for doing so. He knew right then that it was in everyone's best interest to keep his mother circulating.

Standing by an enormous armchair near the kiva fireplace was Franklin Crown-Smith. Franklin stood silently staring into the fire, a double whiskey clutched in his left hand. He appeared to be deep in thought, like an actor preparing mentally for an evening on the stage.

The director had hair an artificial shade of raven black and a long, thin face, tanned brown by the desert sun. Every day he wore the same bolo tie of braided black leather straps tipped in silver spikes, cinched with an obsidian arrowhead concho. Brandon noted how the firelight turned the high bones of Franklin's cheeks and the deep creases around his mouth into craggy, shifting landscapes, leaving him handsome in a way that could only sell a lot of cigarettes. The other artists at the Pembroke seemed to think Franklin was somewhere in his late forties, but no one could really be sure. Brandon made a note to ask his mother's opinion of the man's age when they got home.

Alexandra jabbed Brandon in the ribs with a bony index finger and nodded in Crown-Smith's direction. He took this rather painful bit of sign language to mean that she wanted a formal presentation. He obliged.

"Franklin, I'd like you to meet my mother. She's visiting from Washington, D.C."

"And the world," added Alexandra.

Franklin sighed and turned toward the two of them. Before he could say a word, Alexandra took his right hand in both of hers and held it warmly. "Mr. Crown-Smith," she said, "I hear we have something in common. You're a devotee of Rimsky-Korsakov. I simply adore Rimsky-Korsakov. And his operas … well, they're gems. Unmined gems, don't you agree?"

Franklin simply stared at her and said, "Perhaps."

Brandon rallied to his mother's aid without concern for the truth. "Mom's a great opera fan. Aren't you, Mother? I've often heard her talk about how she felt when she saw The Snow Goose for the first time."

"The Snow Maiden." corrected Alexandra. "Yes, well, Covent Garden was exciting that season all around, but you know," she said, giving Franklin an adoring glance, "a true peak experience was seeing your Native American Turandot at the Kennedy Center."

"That was a long time ago," said Franklin, slowly warming to her. "I'm surprised you remember it."

"Oh, not that long ago, surely," rejoined Brandon's mother. "I remember Opera West! was all anyone talked about at the time in Washington. And with that Hopi Turandot, well, you were the toast of the town."

Franklin gave Brandon a glance that indicated his approval of Alexandra then turned back to her and said, "I hope you're enjoying your stay in Taos."

"Well, I am," she insisted. "It's absolutely breathtaking here." Then Alexandra paused. "Oh dear! I'm sorry. I should have picked some phrase other than 'breathtaking,' now shouldn't I? How thoughtless of me. I was so terribly sorry to learn about what happened to that poor woman who was staying here. Strangled to death. It must be just devastating to have something like this happen! Right here. Amongst you. Do the police have any idea who might have done such a thing?"

"No," said Franklin.

"I wouldn't say that," said a throaty woman's voice. Alexandra and Brandon turned around to see the novelist Glenda Guilder standing directly behind them. Glenda was a bottom-heavy sort of woman with a hairstyle that seemed slightly worse than a home perm and slightly better than shock therapy. She held a shiny new hardback book in her clutches. "They have a few ideas who might have wanted to kill Sienna. At least I gave them a few ideas."

"Really?" Alexandra drawled. "Do you think it was somebody here?"

"S'my mom," introduced Brandon. "Mom, Glenda."

"Hello," said Alexandra.

Before Glenda could reply, Franklin turned on her sternly and snapped, "It's interesting that out of everyone here, the police only questioned you about what happened to Miss Sandoval. Why is that?"

"They didn't call me," she said. "I called them."

Franklin was unimpressed. "That's not what I would have thought." Then he paused and asked, "What did you tell them?"

"I wouldn't worry, Frank. I didn't tell them I knew who killed Sienna, because I don't. I just thought it might be helpful if the police knew some things about her."

"Things. Of course."

"Oh, I know lots of things. Who her friends were. Who her friends weren't. Who she was sleeping with. Things like that. Oh, yes!" she added quickly, looking at Franklin with an accusatory smirk. "And they wanted to know if there was a tall person here who wears a thin leather belt. They didn't say if they had anyone particular in mind."

It took a lot of control for Brandon not to look down at Franklin's waist. Instead, knowing full well he himself fit that sort of vague description, Brandon laughed at Glenda and declared, "I confess! I'm tall! I wear thin leather belts! I wanted her house! I did it!"

Alexandra gave her son a withering look, then unabashedly gave Franklin's belt loops a thorough examination before venturing an opinion. "Just because that poor woman was strangled in a particular way doesn't mean the killer has to be a tall person who wears thin belts. Anyone with a little imagination could have made those same marks on that woman's neck."

"Like how?" asked Glenda.

Alexandra fished in her handbag and pulled out a cloth measuring tape that was rolled up into a little coil. "Kneel down," she said to her, "and I'll show you."

Glenda Guilder was delighted. "You're good! Maybe I should give this to you instead of Frank." She extended the book she held in her hands toward him.

"What is that?" Franklin said suspiciously.

"My new book. I just got the first copies today. It's all on my research into the history of executions. I even interviewed several men currently on death row. The thing I found most amazing was that all killers had a certain 'look.' I think, Franklin, you might find my book … informative."

Glenda remained with the book in her outstretched hand. Franklin did not move. Alexandra started to coo congratulations to Glenda, until she caught a glance at the book's title, Death's Doorstep."

"I don't have time for light reading," Franklin said flatly.

This was just the reaction Glenda wanted. She smiled at him with sweet malice and noted, "Oh, take it anyway. You never know when you'll have time to kill."

Alexandra, Brandon, and especially Franklin were struck dumb. That last statement seemed to visibly upset Frank as beads of perspiration began welling on his upper lip. Glenda did not withdraw either the offending volume or her penetrating stare. She seemed to revel in the unease she was causing.

As if on cue, PopIris Nelson appeared at Glenda's side, diplomatically taking the book from her, tucking it under her skeletal arm. "Glenda, would you like to lend me a hand with the drinks?"

"Love to," she said and let PopIris lead her out of the room.

Franklin watched the women go. "Excuse me," he said with a chilly edge. "I have something to take care of. It was nice to meet you. Enjoy your stay." He turned and followed Iris and Glenda through the door.

Alexandra whispered to Brandon, "She's in love with him."

"WHAT?" he exclaimed quite loudly. Ethan looked up from across the room at the sound of his voice.

Alexandra gave him a look that sternly commanded "Keep your voice down!" then said very slyly, very entre-nous, "That was a jealous woman. It's all over her. She thinks he was having an affair with the dead girl, so she wants to make him pay."

"That's ridiculous. Franklin and Glenda? What could he possibly see in her?"

"I didn't say he was in love with her. I said she was in love with him. I suppose it's understandable. Although he's not warmth incarnate, he is oddly attractive. If I play my cards right, I think he and I could even hit it off."

"Why on Earth would you want to?"

"He's tall, dark, handsome, and wears thin leather belts. I'm almost a divorcee. I have to keep my options open, you know."

"Yeah, right," sighed Brandon. "Just don't make me call him Daddy. And where'd you get all that stuff about the Hopi Turandot?"

"From his biography in the brochure you showed me, of course."

"Oh."

She gave Brandon a picaresque smile and gracefully moved to take a pew next to Moira under an unusually large cow skull. The specter of Alexandra's hairdo superimposed in front of the bones was akin to what a drag queen might envision during a hallucination about Georgia O'Keeffe.

Ethan once again looked up and grinned at Brandon, leaving Brandon torn between wanting to sit near Ethan and odd little P.J. Copeland and feeling obliged to sit next to his mother and Moira.

Before he could make a decision, one was made for him. PopIris returned, bearing a tray with three dry martinis.

She offered him a drink and then suggested they go over and give his mother a quick tour of the room before the opera started. Having heard PopIris' Penitente Room speech several times, Brandon wasn't thrilled with the idea, but couldn't think of an excuse fast enough to avoid hearing it once more.

"You probably think we've led you into a chamber of horrors," PopIris said to Alexandra as she proffered her a martini.

"No, it's charming!" insisted Alexandra as she lifted down her triangular glass and gave it a quick appraisal. "Tanqueray?"

"Bombay."

"What fun," she said, taking a tiny sip and giving a wince of strained delight. "Well! So tell me, why do they have a funeral parlor on the premises?"

"You never know when you'll need one," answered Brandon.

PopIris ignored Brandon and took this as her cue to begin her canned monologue. "Actually this room is supposed to look like a Penitente chapel. Mr. Pembroke was quite insistent that it be authentic and they've done a very good job, don't you think? See the heavy wooden beams across the ceiling? Those are called vigas and their placement and carving is very suggestive of a real Penitente morada."

Brandon started tuning out PopIris' singsong spiel the moment she began. His attention wandered around the room to Ethan and P.J. by the Ansel Adams prints, then to Lorna and Brian by the bookcase, and finally to a yellowing leaf on the geranium centerpiece. Suddenly Franklin came back into the room hot on the trail of the evilly beatific Glenda who was bearing another tray of martinis. Brandon could hear him say, "Come back here," to her, but she ignored him and proceeded to distribute her drinks around the library.

"… were a bizarre offshoot of the Order of Saint Francis of Assisi," continued PopIris. "Even a penitent like St. Francis would have had his blood chilled if he'd have seen the lengths his followers carried his teachings …"

Glenda moved with her tray over to Brian and Lorna. Franklin stopped a few paces away and glared at them all. Glenda handed Lorna a drink, then offered one to Brian. As he reached forward to take his glass, she bent forward and whispered something to him.

"… records show that in the 1800's, nearly every non-Indian New Mexican was not only a Catholic, but also a Penitente …"

Brian's eyes grew wide, then they narrowed. He shot an angry look first at Franklin, then at Lorna. He put his martini back on Glenda's tray, then crossed to confront Franklin.

"... began to flagellate their own bare backs with cactus whips. Up to five hundred lashes. They would increase the blows in intensity while the other followers fell upon their knees, chanting ..."

Brandon could not hear what Brian Epstein said to Franklin, but he could see Franklin was not about to be intimidated. Franklin said something that appeared to be rather cutting in reply as Lorna raced over to stand between them. Brian reached out to poke Franklin in the chest, but Frank grabbed his wrist firmly and held it tight.

"... were so sharp, the entire covering of flesh would be torn off, leaving the bones of the ribs exposed to full view. You can see there in the third painting, one of the self-flagellants with his back ripped ..."

Franklin released his grip on Brian and turned to walk away. Brian said something like "... ever catch you ..." and Franklin stopped, turned back and smirked. This made Brian very angry.

"... behind the cross bearers, and at every step would give vicious blows to the naked backs of the men in front. Behind these would follow a party of about eight more flagellants, followed by a dozen or so men carrying in front of them primitive figures of saints. Here, there's one right there next to you."

Lorna tried to pull Brian away. He said something to Franklin like "... doesn't need your help ..." and the word "operate." At least it sounded to Brandon like the word "operate." Franklin said something in return that caused Brian to cock back his fist in preparation for a sock to the jaw. Lorna had enough. She bustled Franklin out of the room leaving Brian seething in silent rage.

"... and notice the carving along the back of the ... uh, Brandon? Could you turn that over?" continued Glenda.

Brandon hadn't been paying attention and looked down at what he had apparently been holding for some time in his own hands. The gleaming skull of a skeleton nailed to a cross smiled up at him.

"Jesus!" Brandon barked in surprise.

"No, it's just one of the Penitents," said Mother and reached to take the statue from his hands. "Beautiful piece of work, isn't it?"

CHAPTER FOUR

Brandon and Alexandra pressed their noses up against one Plaza shop window after another. They were on the prowl. Alexandra had never traveled anywhere in the world without making at least one significant purchase, so she was aghast to have been in New Mexico for two whole days without even the slightest bit of friction on her credit card. Looking like a pair of modern day hunter-gatherers, the two shoppers skulked around in the shadows successfully avoiding the glare of the midday sun as well as any shop that did not carry the American Express Card sign.

Taos Plaza was small, square, and brown, virtually identical to every other plaza in every other New Mexican town. Cheap souvenir shops, elegant art galleries and sleepy western cafes all huddled together around a brown brick courtyard ringed with low adobe walls. The La Fonda Hotel enticed tourists to the south end of the plaza with signs alluding to a scandalous collection of D.H. Lawrence's little-known paintings. The shops on the west flank had colorful bunches of dried chiles, called ristras, rocking gently in the breeze alongside rainbow wind socks. In fact, just about every shop on the plaza had ristras and wind socks – as well as identical inventories of Taos T-shirts, mock Indian pottery made of molded painted plaster, garish postcards from the 1960s, and plastic Native American turquoise jewelry from Hong Kong, ROC.

Keeping with this tourist-pleasing theme, the Taoseños, in a fit of civic pride, planted hundreds of Holland bulbs at the center of the plaza. The lavish floral display, so welcomed by the tourists of spring, was unfortunately an eyesore to the tourists of summer. By June, the daffodils and tulips clumped by the painted wrought iron benches were a sorry sight, their gangly yellow stems holding only crispy brown heads. Like the flowers, summer afternoons on the plaza were dead, dry and quiet, too. The only sounds in the air came from the cottonwood trees above, alive with the laughing of magpies.

"What do you think of this one?" Alexandra asked while pointing to a bluish sand painting of the Indian deity Kokopelli in the window of a drug store.

"Oh, come on," Brandon said with wrinkled nose. "Do be serious."

"Well, I rather like it," she insisted. "It's got fire. It's got movement. I think it's got some potential."

"It's also got matching salt and pepper shakers."

Her eyes lit up. "Really? Where?"

He pulled her away from the window. "Never mind," he said. "Let's try this place over here." They walked over to a rather squashed looking storefront that specialized in wood statues and camera film. In the display case were seven small Penitente carvings, scary little knock-offs of the ones in the Pembroke collection. "My god, these guys are everywhere!" Brandon exclaimed.

"Now, isn't it wonderful?" Alexandra mused. "Before last evening, I wouldn't have known a thing about these little carvings. Now I can practically teach a course on the Penitente sect and all its masochistic arts. So what do you think? Should I buy a bleeding Jesus for over my bed?"

"Why don't you just wait and I'll paint you one on black velvet," Brandon offered.

"No," said his mother with much too much seriousness, "it's got to be authentic. Last night, Miss Popeye insisted that these were powerful symbols, not to be taken lightly."

Brandon gave the dripping Savior another look and scowled. "I didn't think you were listening to PopIris last night," he said. "I know I wasn't. I was trying too hard to eavesdrop on all the little dramas going on across the room."

"Oh, that?" sighed Alexandra. "Well, if he's really all that jealous a person, it seems odd that he hasn't made an effort to marry her."

"Wha–who?" he stammered. "Who do you mean?"

"I thought you were eavesdropping."

"I was, but I couldn't hear much with that woman rattling on in my ear about self-flagellation. You couldn't have heard any more than I did."

His mother looked surprised. "Of course I could. That woman with the dark hair … Laura?"

"Lorna."

"Well, she was caught by the heavy novel woman …"

"Glenda."

"Glenda. That's what I said. Glenda apparently caught Lorna in the act of doing something unseemly – I'm not quite sure what – with the portentous Franklin Crown-Smith. You kind of wonder what would possess a beautiful girl like that to get herself in a clinch with a man that strange."

"You said you were attracted to him," noted Brandon.

"Yes, but I'm strange, too. Then again, I suppose from what the curly-haired gentleman …"

"Brian."

"… said, she hoped for some sort of assistance in getting her opera produced."

Brandon was impressed. "How could you hear any of that?"

"It's an old trick I learned," said Alexandra, "from going to all those awful embassy dinners."

"Embassy dinners, huh?" he said in a tone rarely used on people not suffering from fever.

"Oh yes," continued his mother as they strolled along the plaza. "I would always get stuck with some sort of admiral or other in one corner of the room – either that or it would be someone related to Buddha, you know the type – and I would miss out on all the little intrigues of the evening. Entire political coups would pass me by. Later people would say to me, 'Isn't it horrible? The Grand Pooh-bah is ruined!' or something like that, and I'd feel like I wasn't even there! I would get very upset. Then your father taught me this wonderful technique." Alexandra covered one eye and comically cocked an ear. Brandon noticed people were starting to stare at them. "You keep one eye and ear trained on the boring old coot directly in front of you. With your leftover faculties you zero in on whatever else interests you in the room, and then filter, filter, filter!"

"You what?"

"Filter, dear. You freeze a very intelligent look on your face, listen to all conversations possible at once, then filter out the hogwash. Really, you just discard 90 percent of what is foisted on you in the name of cocktail conversation. And since you're not saying a word, people think you're the most divine thing to walk upon the Earth since Elvis."

Of course Brandon had never heard of anything so ridiculous in his life, but she did seem to have a handle on what Brian and Franklin argued about the night before, so he humored her. "What else did you glean from the babble?" he inquired with interest.

"GooGoo L'Amour had an expensive lunch. The boy with the southern accent is from Kentucky. And the balding gentleman has a spastic colon."

Apparently even Moira, P.J. Copeland and Ethan Arnold were not immune from her radar. "So tell me about these embassy dinners," Brandon said to her. "Where was this?"

"I can't say."

"You mean you've forgotten?"

"No, I mean I can't say." His mother gave him one of those "enough said" looks and pulled out a hairpin. She stuck the pin in her mouth while she tamed a few wild locks on the back of her head. After using her teeth and fingers to pry the free hairpin open, she deftly and swiftly slipped the bobby homeward. Brandon let the embassy matter rest.

The two of them did one more lap around the plaza just so Alexandra could re-examine an overpriced kachina, then steered themselves back in the direction of the Pembroke. The black and white magpies in the trees overhead cheered their exit.

Brandon's mother had worn the wrong type of shoes for walking in Taos. The Taoseño sidewalks were quirkily unassertive, meekly following the rolling lay of the land. The constant up- and downhill progress of a Taos pedestrian almost demanded a pair of hiking boots, not a pair of sling-backs with three inch heels. Alexandra soon developed the stately gate of a woman who looks fabulous at the price of great pain. Consequently, they walked slowly and stopped often.

Two houses from Brandon's studio, they came upon Ethan Arnold (Beautiful Ethan, thought Brandon. How could she refer to him as the balding gentleman with the spastic colon?) kneeling down in his flower garden. Although the Casa Grande had well-tended flower and cactus gardens on all sides, the individual artist cottages were left completely un-landscaped. Only natural New Mexican flora grew around the artists' houses. Ethan distinguished himself from the rest by cultivating quite a respectable little patch of flowering bushes, strangely clipped greenery, and assorted dangerous-looking poppies. Brandon's mother seized upon this chance meeting to allow her feet to rest a moment.

"What a priceless little garden!" gushed Alexandra. "Brandon, do we have a camera handy? Do get out your camera sweetheart and take my picture in front of this lovely little patch."

Brandon did not have a camera handy, nor was he ready to beg, borrow or steal one to take her picture. He could tell she wasn't serious. His mother was just buttering Ethan up before talking him to death.

"You don't have to do that," said Ethan in his very soft voice. "If you need any pictures, I've got thousands of them."

"Well, of course that's right. You're a photographer, aren't you?"

"Hi, Ethan," said Brandon.

"Hello, Brandon," he replied. "Shopping?"

"We did our best," sighed Alexandra, "but the Muse of Purchase did not smile. May I?" she said and hobbled over to sit on his front step. Ethan reached over and unfolded a small lawn chair that was leaning against the house. Alexandra gurgled and thanked him profusely and then plopped herself down and kicked off her shoes.

Brandon could tell Ethan had been working hard all morning. Mottled patches of sweat matted down his chest hair in spots. His fringe of strawberry hair was also wet and curling on the back of his neck.

Alexandra cooed over the flowers and set down pronouncements about the weather before getting down to serious gossip. "Wasn't it a shame we didn't get to hear the opera last night?" she said. "I was so looking forward to hearing what Mr. Crown-Smith had chosen. The Death of Hope, wasn't that it? Wasn't that what we were supposed to hear?"

"Probably," said Ethan. "He played it last year, I think. All those obscure German operas sound alike to me."

"So, you've been here before?" said Alexandra with a squeal in her voice. "How wonderful. I'm sure if I were ever chosen to come here, I would die to come back again and again."

"It's all right," shrugged Ethan.

Brandon's mother rubbed her feet and leaned forward. "Has anyone else been here before?" she asked in Brandon's general direction.

"I don't know," Brandon replied, even though he knew the question was not meant for him.

"Lorna," replied Ethan after a thoughtful pause. "Lorna was here last year, too."

"Such a shame about last night!" Alexandra said. "She seemed so upset by something, poor dear." Brandon and his mother both peered intently at Ethan to see if this last comment would have any effect on him. It didn't. "Do you have any idea what was bothering her so?"

"No," said Ethan with all the emotion of a sphinx.

"Well, it is none of my business, I admit," she continued, "but I admit my curiosity was piqued. Could you make out anything that her gentleman friend and Franklin were arguing about?"

"No," he said again. Ethan would have made a terrible talk show guest.

"That's too bad. Such a little drama! Well anyway, it was exciting just the same." Alexandra straightened out the folds in her skirt and took a moment to regroup. "Perhaps tonight will be just as exciting. You're coming, aren't you, Mr. Arnold?"

Ethan finally showed a little surprise. "Coming where?" he asked.

"I was told we're having an evening of food and art. It sounded delightful. I do hope you're coming."

"Was that tonight?" he said with a sigh. "I completely forgot. I don't have anything to bring."

"Don't worry about it," Brandon reassured him. "Everyone's bringing lots of food. Just pick up a pack of tortillas and a jug of wine and you'll be fine. Oh, and bring some slides of your photos if you've got them."

"Oh, do!" encouraged Alexandra. "How wonderful. I just can't wait. By the way, where is this going to be?"

"At Lorna's," Brandon said.

"Where's that?"

Ethan brushed the dirt from his knees and nodded at the house next door. "Right there," he said.

Alexandra gave the house a thorough inspection without even leaving her chair. "Well yes, I should have guessed. I can see the grand piano in the front window from here. She's a composer, isn't she? That's what they said. Working on an opera. Wonderful, how exciting! You must be able to hear her practicing. After all, her piano's practically in your garden."

"I listen to her all the time," said Ethan. "Lorna plays beautifully."

"But it must bother you when you're trying to work."

"No, not really. I don't need that kind of concentration. That's why they sandwich musical people in between two visual artists."

"Yeah, my house is on the other side of her," Brandon added. "We don't need the kind of silence, say, a novelist does."

"I see," said Alexandra. "It's all so well thought out. Brandon! You never told me you could hear Lorna playing."

"I can't," he said. "Her front room faces Ethan's garden. I can't hear a thing."

"I hear everything that goes on between them at Lorna's," said Ethan.

Alexandra took the bait. "Them?"

"Her and Brian. They've got separate houses, but he sleeps over at her house. They fought all night last night."

"They fought with Crown-Smith at the lecture and then fought with each other when they got home? Well! What were they fighting about?"

"I don't know," said Ethan.

"Weren't you listening?" Brandon's mother pumped on.

Ethan paused. "No," he said.

"Yes, well of course," she sighed as a limp lock of hair fell like a noodle between her eyes.

Ethan clarified, "I was working in the darkroom at the time."

"So late at night?"

"That's when it's darkest," Ethan answered simply. He picked up a watering can that was lying nearby and began to sprinkle his flowers.

Alexandra could tell she wasn't going to get any more of Ethan's parched form of gossip, so she steered the conversation toward the home stretch. "Well, you'll have to bring lots of pictures for us tonight. Do you have any of the garden here? I'd love to see them."

"I'll bring slides of Montana," said Ethan. "You're welcome to come over any time you want to see the rest."

"Delightful," said Alexandra. She rose and wiggled slightly in her shoes to see if her feet still hurt. "I'll be over every day." Ethan smiled like someone who thought the woman was exaggerating.

As Brandon and Alexandra were turning to leave, they caught sight of Glenda Guilder trundling toward them down the drive. Glenda, wearing sunglasses, a wide-brimmed hat and an expression fecund with the promise of information, looked for all the world to Brandon like a big bag of gossip who was about to explode. From the hungry look that stole across Alexandra's face, he knew his mother had somewhat the same impression of her, too.

Of course Glenda had also seen the three of them. That afternoon, however, she was apparently on a mission to spread much more than just raw data to the neighborhood. Glenda was burgeoning with gleeful ill-will, and this time Ethan Arnold was her intended target.

Making a bee-line for Ethan in his garden, she hiked her oversized PBS tote bag high on her shoulder sending a mass of bangle bracelets clanging up around her pudgy elbow. "Boy are you in trouble!" she announced the split second she was within earshot. On her way past Alexandra, she managed to pop off a quick, "Hello, Mrs. uh …"

"Call me Alexandra."

"Hiya, Lexy. So, Ethan …"

Ethan instinctively put down his watering can, picked up his hoe and held it defensively across his chest. "What?" he said.

"I just came from the Big House and Casanova's on the warpath. He wants you out of here and now!"

Ethan did not react in any way but stood there silent and defiant. Brandon, on the other hand, was stunned by this announcement.

"B-b-but … why?" he stuttered. "What's wrong?"

Glenda remained focused on Ethan. "I was in the Penitente Room going though some books," she said, "and I heard Franklin in his office screaming at PopIris about your garden. I guess somebody tipped him off at what you've got going out here. I don't know how he never noticed before, but you should've moved your plants around the back of your house where Franklin wouldn't have been able to see them."

"There's not enough sun back there," said Ethan.

"Well, he's going to get you evicted on a technicality, because you can't have a garden at the Pembroke."

Not quite understanding Glenda's agitation or Franklin's floraphobia, Alexandra interrupted and inquired, "Why not?

What could possibly be wrong with growing a few flowers? They're lovely."

"Well, it ain't the damned flowers he's worried about!" cackled Glenda.

"It's the water," Ethan interjected. Water is very expensive here and they don't want us to waste it."

Brandon nodded. "Yeah, they say that on the rule sheet."

"But he can't use that as an excuse because I'm using only grey water out here."

Alexandra looked at Brandon. "Grey water? What is that? Radioactive?"

"That would be heavy water," Brandon said. "Grey water is recycled waste water."

"Oh."

Glenda shook her head superciliously. "He doesn't care. PopIris is trying to talk him out of it, but Frankie's got a big hair up his butt about you. He said he never wanted you here in the first place, and now he's got a good reason to let you go! It looks like you're history."

Ethan just looked Glenda in the eye and said, "I don't think so," then he turned and handed his hoe to Brandon. "Excuse me," he said to Alexandra and went inside the house. The screen door closed with a bang.

"Poor Ethan," sighed Glenda. "I didn't want to upset him. I just thought he should know what was going on. You don't think he'll take this news lying down, do you?"

"I don't know," said Brandon.

"Well, thank goodness he has someone as reliable as you to tell him about it," remarked Alexandra. "Not many people would have the courage to inform a friend of his impending eviction. And not many people would have the remarkable hearing it would take to learn the news in the first place."

Glenda's brow furrowed. "Excuse me?" she asked.

"Last night, I noticed during our visit to the main house that the offices were right there in the front of the building, while that Penitente morgue was way, way far in the back. With those thick mud walls in between you and Mr. Crown-Smith, combined with all that distance, you must have phenomenal hearing, Miss Goulden!"

"Guilder," she corrected. "It's so nice to see you again, Lexy. Where are you staying?"

"Why right here ..."

Brandon cut his mother off. "... in Taos at the Sagebrush Inn!" he lied. Glenda nodded her approval and said her goodbyes. Once she was safely out of earshot, Brandon turned and scowled at Alexandra. "You didn't have to insult her. She was just trying to be helpful to Ethan."

"Well, I didn't mean to be rude, but it just doesn't make much sense now, does it? This is a beautiful garden! I just don't understand."

"He's breaking the rules."

"Oh, pooh on the rules!" said his mother. "You're breaking the rules. I'm breaking the rules. And don't think I didn't notice that you suspect that woman of being Franklin's little tattletale. The Sagebrush Inn indeed! What I suspect is more likely is that this garden is the least of Franklin's concerns."

"Well, Moira did tell me Franklin always had it in for Ethan. Franklin only let him come back because the Ansel Adams Society has him cataloging Pembroke's stash of Adams photographs over at the Big House. Ethan's some sort of bigwig in the Adams Society, I guess."

"Well that's interesting," said Alexandra, brightening a little. "Do they keep all of the photos displayed over there or ..."

Their conversation was cut short by the approach of a dented green pickup truck traveling at high speed up the drive. The horn blared twice in warning as the driver aimed right for Brandon and Alexandra.

The mother and son froze in fear like a pair of highway deer. Leaving them no time to either move out of the way or make their peace with God, the driver approached within inches of Brandon and his mother, then swerved and slammed on the brakes at the last second, enveloping them all in a cloud of red dust.

As the air cleared and his heart started beating once more, Brandon furiously stomped over to the door of the truck and opened it with a violent jerk. He was just about to drag the crazy driver out onto the dirt drive and punch him in the face, when Moira Atchison's big grin and distinctive laugh hit him first.

"Hello, Brando!" she yodeled. "Scared ya, huh? So how do you like my new truck? Pretty cool, don't you think?"

Brandon couldn't decide how to respond. He was torn between laughing at her for buying that abomination of a truck, or scolding her for giving him heart failure. "Jesus!" was all that came out of his mouth.

"So you like it?" she said. "I knew you would. Three hundred dollars. What a deal!"

"Don't do that again," Brandon ordered.

"Sorry," Moira chattered cheerfully on, "I was just so excited about my new truck I had to show you right away! Isn't it wonderful?"

"GooGoo!" greeted Alexandra coming around the front of the truck, "What a surprise. You certainly are one for theatrical entrances."

"Howdy-doo, Zanderoo. Wanna go for a ride?"

Brandon saw the look on his mother's face and couldn't tell which troubled her more: the prospect of being referred to forever in the future as "Zanderoo," or the prospect of a ride in that truck. He braced himself for what undoubtedly would be the curtest refusal in history, but his mother's reply came as a complete shock.

"I'd love to," she said. "I haven't driven in a 1957 Chevy since, well … 1957! You'll have to let me ride in the back."

Brandon stared agape, first at his mother, and then at the pickup. Sure enough, the truck was circa sometime in the late 'fifties. Its forest green sides were rusted through in places and the entire front bumper was missing. In the bed of the truck were a tool box, some long leather straps, and two large bales of hay which Brandon tried to imagine his mother riding on. The thought of Alexandra in the back of the truck, sitting on top of a bale of hay, holding onto her hair for dear life was too much for even Brandon's ample imagination.

"Whose tools are all those?" he asked.

"Mine!" beamed Moira. "I love my tools, gotta have my tools! You gotta see me. I get my tool belt. Strap that thing on. Get that butt-crack thing going around the back there. Makes me feel like a real American, Brando!" She burst into peals of laughter. "So what do you say? Hop in, we'll go for a ride!"

"No, thanks. We've got too much to do this afternoon. Are you ready for tonight?"

"What, the pot luck?"

"Yes," said Brandon. "I was going to ask if you could come over and help me make the enchiladas later. I don't even know where to begin."

"Yes, do come over," said Alexandra. "In fact, let's have lunch first right now. It's long past my lunch time and I've got to eat something. I'm hyperglycemic, you know."

"Since when?" asked Brandon.

"Since now. My blood sugar is low anyway and now I'm feeling a little faint. My blood sugar has completely run out. I need to eat something."

Knowing full well she meant HYPOglycemic and that real HYPERglycemics have anything but low blood sugar, Brandon deferred to his mother's self-diagnosis and urged Moira to join them for lunch.

Moira climbed back into the cab of her truck. "Sorry, Brando. No can do. I'm going for a quick spin and then I got a hundred sopaipillas to fry! I'll see you tonight at the soiree."

"Wait!" he called to her as she revved up the engine. "What am I supposed to do about enchiladas?"

"Piece of cake," she shouted over the roar of the engine. "Just clean out your refrigerator. Anything that's solid, wrap in a tortilla. Anything that's liquid, pour on the top ... then hide everything under cheese!"

"But ..."

She waved and floored the accelerator, kicking up another cloud of red dirt. "Bye!"

Alexandra and Brandon watched Moira go and coughed a little from the dust in her wake. Alexandra turned to her son and said, "I wonder what the hay was for?"

"The hay in the back of the truck?" Brandon asked and then shrugged. "I don't know. In Taos it's standard equipment on every pickup truck."

"I see," said Alexandra, turning for home. "Now what are we going to do about lunch?"

"How about peanut butter and jelly with a shot of insulin?" he offered.

"How about going to a nice restaurant? My treat," she countered. "We'll just sit someplace nice and quiet the entire afternoon and maybe even bribe the kitchen staff to make you your, your ... what was that thing you were going to cook?"

"Enchiladas."

"Well, whatever they are, we'll buy them. How does that sound?"

"It's a deal," said Brandon, who hated cooking anyway. "I won't tell anyone if you won't."

"Deal," said Alexandra, who did an about-face and pointed herself back toward town. Suddenly she stopped and listened. "Do you hear that?" she asked her son.

Brandon paused a moment, then looked over at Lorna Shaw's window. He could see Lorna playing the piano with the afternoon sun spilling through the glass like a spotlight on her face. Alexandra reached over and held her son by the hand. Brandon gave his mother's hand a small squeeze and the two of them stood in the garden and listened to Lorna as she played a melancholy song.

The music came into the garden loud and clear.

CHAPTER FIVE

"Answer the door, dammit."

For perhaps the first time in either of their lives, Brandon and Alexandra were actually early for something. They stood on Lorna's doorstep precariously balancing large aluminum foil pans of restaurant-made enchiladas for the pot luck. Alexandra, sporting a small white jacket over a white silk dress, took the precaution of wearing oven mitts and an apron since the pan's orange-red sauce had a tendency to slosh and drip. Brandon, on the other hand, had not the forethought to protect either his hands or his clothes. Holding his enchilada pan by the very tips of his fingers to avoid getting burnt, he was left with little recourse but to attempt to knock on Lorna's front door with his elbow.

And knock he did. And again and again. The sound of a vacuum cleaner whining inside set the two of them to fantasizing that their knocking would never be heard, leaving them to drip and burn on the purgatory of Lorna's porch. Brandon pounded one last time with the side of his elbow and knocked his funny bone so hard it brought tears to his eyes.

"Isn't there a doorbell?" asked Alexandra.

"No, there isn't a doorbell," growled Brandon in pain. "It's an artist studio, not a tract house."

"Well, in my experience, wherever there's a door, there's usually a doorbell."

"Well, there's not one here. Franklin had them all removed."

"What on Earth for?"

"Mother," he sighed, "if you're in the middle of producing some kind of art, the last thing you want to hear is the Avon Lady."

"Well I consider that absolutely Communist."

"Communist?"

"It's positively un-American to discourage shopping in any shape or form," said Alexandra.

Brandon started banging on the door with his head – partly to be heard inside and partly for the dramatic effect. The sound of the vacuum ceased and Brian Epstein opened the door. Dizzy from near concussion, Brandon stumbled through the portal nearly dropping his pan in the process.

"Well, hello," said Brian. "You're early."

Alexandra proffered her enchiladas and gave Brian an apologetic smile. "We wanted to get our little pans of, of ... whatever you call these messy little things over here ... before the crowd could possibly jostle us into disaster. I hope it's no problem," she said.

"No, not at all. We're just running around here, trying to get the place cleaned up."

"Well, I'd love to help, but I'm simply not dressed for it. Here, would you mind?" Alexandra said handing Brian the overflowing pan of enchiladas. "They're still warm, but maybe you should keep them in the oven. Thank you ever so much." Brian awkwardly took the tray with a confused half-grin and walked slowly toward the kitchen like a new waitress delivering her first cup of coffee.

Moira, it appeared, was early, too. She was in the kitchen with Lorna, holding a very loud conversation over the drone of the stove exhaust fan. Lorna darted back and forth like a woman possessed, her hair a wild mass of root-beer-colored tangles barely kept in check with a hastily tied hair band. A knee-length apron (stained with, of all things, blue spots) covered grey shorts and sweatshirt. She looked tired and nervous, but did a remarkable job of keeping up with her end of the cheerful kitchen shouting match.

Moira, on the other hand, looked like the opening scene of Macbeth, cussing and stirring a large crackling kettle of boiling oil. Brandon remembered she was supposedly making sopaipillas that evening. The doughnut-like bread puffs she was trying to replicate were a New Mexico delicacy. In Taos, they were served with butter and honey at practically all meals because their oily texture quenched the fire from even the hottest of chile peppers. The mark of any New Mexican chef was the quality of his sopaipillas. From the epithets he heard her shout from the stove, Brandon gathered that Moira was missing that particular mark.

With the enchiladas safely in the oven, Lorna ushered Brandon and Alexandra into the front room and offered them a drink. On their decline of refreshment, she plopped herself into an overstuffed chair and threw her apron over her head. "I always do this!" she moaned.

"We're so sorry we're early," purred Alexandra.

"No, it's not you," said Lorna, coming out from under her apron. "I was in Santa Fe all day today and farted around until the last possible minute before I even started to drive back, so it serves me right everyone's here early. Poor Brian. I just called him up fifteen minutes ago, practically in tears because I hadn't done any vacuuming ... well, I hadn't done shit that's what I hadn't done. So I've got him working now. Moira came over a half hour ago with all that boiling oil shit so I'm not even going to start to clean the kitchen even though there's all this shit that has to be done. I must be tired. I'm saying shit an awful lot, huh? Well, shit. Anyway ... are you sure I can't get you anything?"

"Why don't give us some little tasks to do, and then you go get ready?" offered Alexandra. "I'm not dressed to do any cleaning, but I can set out little wootsie plates or forks or punch cups or whatever you need."

Lorna heaved a sigh. "That would be fantastic. Thank you. I really need to hop in the bathtub for a few minutes before all the rest get here. It drives me crazy that there's no shower. Washing your hair in a bathtub is next to impossible."

"Yes, I know," said Alexandra. "When we lived in Greece, I had to wash my hair in the Adriatic, isn't that right, Brandon?"

Brandon just stared at his mother then said. "You should go look at Lorna's bathroom."

"It's awful," said Lorna.

"An old tub with rust stains, a toilet tank way up in the air, a trap door in the floor and a window in the ceiling. It's like a surrealist painting."

"And no air, Brandon."

"And no air. Mom's right, Lorna. Go take a bath, we'll help Brian finish straightening up before the rest get here … even though almost everyone's here already. Did you invite Frank?"

Lorna stood up and released her hair band. "Of course I did."

"And is he coming?"

"Of course he's not," she said. "We're not really speaking right at the moment, Franklin and I, so he's keeping his distance. As well he'd better, if he knows what's good for him."

Alexandra added, "What about Miss Popeye – you know, Miss Nelson?"

"PopIris?" said Lorna with a snort. "Yeah, right. Anyway …" She turned and left the room.

Brandon and Alexandra busied themselves with a very minimal amount of party preparation tasks. Brian Epstein put the vacuum cleaner away and dashed home quickly to grab his portion of the meal and slides of his sculptures. Moira spit curses on the boiling oil. All in all, the little adobe house hummed with industry awaiting the arrival of the last three guests.

Ethan Arnold and Glenda Guilder both arrived close to 7:30, as did Brian Epstein with his load. Dusk had fallen on the house and Alexandra lit the candles surrounding the perfect buffet table setting she had arranged during Lorna's bath. For the centerpiece, she had gathered long sprigs of sagebrush from the back porch and added them to a tall vase of dried flowers Lorna kept high on a dusty shelf. The red paper napkins were laid out in a geometrically perfect half circle around the base of the vase, with a black plastic fork radiating from the center of each napkin. The sunburst effect Alexandra created was credited to an Italian designer she had gone skiing with … presumably at the same time she skied with the Pope.

Brandon slipped into the kitchen to have a chance to talk with Moira privately for the first time since his mother arrived. She was in the middle of lifting the final sopaipilla out of the fry vat with a slotted spoon. Remembering how Moira nearly scared him to death earlier, Brandon decided to get even. He crept up behind her and, with his fingertips, gently squeezed her in the ribs.

There were a crash, a jangle, and a hiss as Moira jumped in fright, hurling her spoon up in the air over their heads. The spoon came down with a whap and a clamor on the floor across the kitchen. Tossed with the spoon, a little sopaipilla gave an almost imperceptible sigh as it deflated on the wall to which it stuck. Moira turned around, wide-eyed with a look of alarm that instantly turned to ire.

"Don't do that!" she snapped.

"I'm sorry I'm sorry," apologized Brandon, trying to squelch his impulse to laugh at her burlesque fright reflex. "I just wanted to talk to you."

"Where'd it go?" said Moira, looking around her on the floor.

"Where'd what go?"

"The last sopaipilla. I had it here on the end of my spoon and … oh, for god's sake." Together they spotted the little fried bread clinging to the wall. Moira knit her brow, then marched over to the sopaipilla and peeled it gingerly from the adobe plaster. She dusted it off and, to Brandon's surprise, bit the tip off one corner. Holding the flattened bread by the edge and blowing into the open tip, she re-inflated it like a balloon. Gently, she placed it at the very top of her serving tray, being careful to hide the nibbled corner from view.

Brandon winced and said, "That's disgusting. Why'd you do that?"

"'Cause it was the best of the bunch," she replied, and from looking at the misshapen lumps on the platter before him, he had to admit it was true.

"Are you quite through?"

"Yep," she said and turned off the propane burner on the stove. "So how's your Mom?"

"Indefatigable."

"Excuse me?"

"Kryptonite wouldn't stop her," he said.

"How's it working out, her staying with you?"

Brandon shrugged. "It's all right. I can stand it, I guess. I want to tell you, I'm a little disappointed that they don't enforce the no-guest policy here, though. What do you do whenever your family comes to town?"

"It's no problem," she said. "I don't have a family."

"What do you mean you don't have a family?"

"I mean I don't have a family. They're all dead. Well, I think I have an aunt or something somewhere down south, but my folks passed away a long while back and my sister Maria died a few years ago."

"Maria? Moira and Maria? What were you, twins?"

Moira laughed. "God, no! She was older than me. We looked a lot alike, but we were like night and day. Maria was like this really straight, really religious opera singer type ... and then there was me, running around naked, tearing poultry apart on stage in front of strangers. Our parents wanted us to be actresses, so I guess it was like this classic case of tears being shed over answered prayers."

Brandon leaned up against the kitchen table and glanced at the slowly sinking plate of sopaipillas. "Why did they want you to be an actress?"

Moira started to funnel the left over oil back into the bottle. "Mom was like this old movie buff," she said. "She named us after ... God, who was it? I don't know ... Maria Montez and Moira whoever that was in The Red Shoes. Maria, they were real proud of. You know, she sang at the New York City Opera and everything. I'm the one that gave the whole family fits. And, you know, till the day she died, my mother never forgave either one of us for not becoming movie stars."

"It could still happen."

Moira rolled her eyes back and shook her head at God. "Or a ballerina or a fairy princess," she said. She smiled and picked up her plate of sopaipillas. "Come on into the party, Brandon, and join the rest of us in the real world."

The front room was alive with the low rumble of conversation, broken occasionally by the light sounds of laughter and various cooing sounds issuing from Alexandra. A portable radio was tuned to a local Spanish language station playing Mexican remakes of American pop tunes.

The food on display was a wild and varied assortment of goods, each indicative of the personality of the provider. Moira, of course, had her freeform, mutant sopaipillas and the Benningtons their tasteful, catered fare. Brian Epstein brought a soup kettle full of sangria and made a firebird ice sculpture to sit in the middle of it. Glenda Guilder assembled a taboulli salad; Lorna baked a chocolate cake; and Ethan Arnold brought seven cans of refried beans and an inexplicable photograph (which turned out to be a close-up of a blue corn tortilla).

Brandon joined his mother as she watched Glenda build a fire in the corner fireplace. Alexandra had obviously been pumping the poor woman for gossip all the time Brandon was in the kitchen with Moira, and as it turned out, she found in Glenda a willing informant.

"Well he's got a reputation with women, I can say that much," Glenda was saying. "It's gotten him in trouble in the past, so I guess that's why we all have to watch our backs now, Lorna, Moira, and me. He tried putting the moves on me, you know."

Brandon instantly assumed that Glenda was talking about Franklin and instantly concluded any such "moves" to be a bunch of wishful thinking on her part. Glenda was the type of woman that could only be considered sexually irresistible if she were stranded on a desert island with an all-male shipwreck. Even then, the cabin boy might turn out to be more popular.

Glenda lowered her voice and continued, "And you know he's sleeping with Lorna, right? It's been going on now for weeks."

"She is here with her husb –, or whatever you call the man when you're not married to him," said Alexandra equally hushed. "They're a couple, aren't they?"

Brandon looked around and whispered, "Who are you guys talking about?"

"You," teased Alexandra.

"Crown-Smith," said Glenda. "You know that's not really his name either, right?"

Alexandra leaned in. "I didn't know that. What is his real name?"

"Something Spanish, I don't know. He tries to pass himself off as Anglo, but I heard he's from some Mexican family over in Farmington."

"Oh, really?"

Brandon nodded in agreement. "Yeah, I heard that, too."

"How very interesting," said Alexandra. "So what was this trouble he's been in with women in the past?"

"Well, I heard two years ago that ..." Glenda stopped in mid-sentence.

Lorna appeared behind Brandon and Alexandra bearing glasses of sangria. "What's going on in this little corner?" she said with mock seriousness. "You three look like thieves plotting a crime. Sangria?"

"Thank you, sweetheart," said Alexandra, taking a glass. "I'm getting filled in on all the deepest secrets of your little colony. Miss Guilder had promised to reveal to me the dark underbelly of the Pembroke."

Lorna smirked. "There's only one dark underbelly you'll find around here, and he's not here tonight."

"Miss Guilder tells me Crown-Smith is not his real name."

"Of course not," said Lorna. "It's Corona."

"Spanish for crown," mused Brandon.

Lorna finished handing out the wine as she spoke. "He added the 'hyphen Smith' so people would think he was British or something. Like any fool would mistake him for British. Anyway ... you have enough wood, Glenda?"

"I think so. Is the flue open?"

Lorna shrugged. "I don't know. We'll find out soon enough, won't we? Anyway ..." Lorna wandered off with her tray to service the rest of the guests.

"Aren't we still missing someone?" asked Alexandra. "That very quiet boy, the poet?"

"P.J." said Brandon. "I wonder where he is. Normally, he wouldn't come to something like this, but he and Ethan are pretty close. I would have assumed they'd arrive together."

Lorna rapped with a metal spoon on the sangria pot to get everyone's attention. "Dig in!" she shouted. Of course no one moved right away for fear of being perceived as overly eager, but as soon as Ethan (who was closest to the table) picked up a paper plate, it was like locusts descending.

Alexandra filled her plate with one tiny spoonful of each dish and made a small nest for herself in a chair near Lorna and Brian and the fire. Brandon checked his initial urge to sit on the floor at his mother's feet as he did when he was a boy. She would have loved that, but among his colleagues it hardly seemed prudent. He instead chose to eat near Ethan, Moira, and Glenda on the opposite side of the room.

Ethan and Glenda started off by swapping war stories of other artist colonies they had known across the country. Moira countered with the horrors and indignities that are suffered by her theatre company in New York's Bowery. The worst thing Brandon could think of to tell them was the time in Philadelphia was when two thieves unknowingly broke in on him while he was examining a severed head – and they all three fainted in fright.

It was well after 8:30 when P.J. Copeland finally showed up for the party. His straw coloured hair was in disarray and he carried a bottle of Jack Daniels in a brown paper bag which he presented to Lorna. Ostensibly, the bourbon was his addition to the pot luck, but the bottle had been opened and a healthy dose of liquor was missing. Brandon presumed from the waver in P.J.'s gate, the dose was only recently administered.

P.J. sat next to Ethan. The two exchanged glances and P.J. responded with a small shrug. When they got up to go to the buffet table, Brandon followed them without their notice. Using his mother's "filter-filter-filter" technique, he tried to appear interested in what was going on in his mother's corner while he shamelessly eavesdropped on the new arrival.

"So, how'd it go?" he heard Ethan ask P.J.

"I don't know," was the reply.

"Did anybody see you?"

"No. I couldn't do it."

"Why not?"

"I got too nervous. I told you I couldn't do it. Leave me alone," said P.J. as he went over to Moira and Glenda with Ethan close in tow.

Brandon had little time to ponder the meaning of that brief exchange, for Lorna had seated herself at the piano to begin the evening's round of entertainment. She announced that they were about to hear a selection from an opera she was currently working on, entitled Long Moon Woman, based on a short story by a local female writer. Lorna played and sang the heroine's aria from the beginning of the second act.

The song told of a woman who gave her body to a judge so he would spare the life of her lover, and then was rejected by her lover because she was untrue. Lorna did not have the most polished of singing voices, still her pitch was perfect and her tone was appropriately dusky. Her throaty voice painfully evoked the torment the Indian maiden was feeling. Brandon was impressed and deeply moved. Alexandra, by the fire, was awash with tears.

The song ended and was followed by a moment of reflective "mm's" from the group and a spattering of grateful applause. Alexandra clapped the loudest and cried the hardest of anyone, then asked Lorna to tell them how the opera ended.

"To win back the love of her man," said Lorna simply, "the woman murders the judge." There were nods of approval and several "oh, wow's" from around the room.

Next on the bill was Moira with her tribute to Hedda Nussbaum. As promised earlier, she performed a wild one-woman re-enactment of domestic violence, chanting and flogging herself while wearing an enormous cone-breasted bra and a handlebar moustache. Sound effects and discordant music were provided by a portable cassette recorder. The finale consisted of fountains of fake blood squirting from the nipples of the bra into Moira's face and hair.

Needless to say, the reactions of the party guests were a bit different this time. The silence and "oh, wow's" that greeted Moira's piece took on a different meaning than they had with Lorna's. Eyes and mouths agape were the initial reactions she received, but Alexandra came through to save the day. Rising from her chair, she led the group in giving Moira a standing ovation.

Moira bowed and bowed and bowed, then asked Lorna if she might take a quick dip in the tub to wash the blood off of her. Lorna gladly acquiesced and helped usher Moira, her tape recorder, and all her bloody props to the bathroom.

Glenda jumped up next as they all sat listening to the sound of the water fill Moira's bath. "I've deliberated long and hard about this," she said while retrieving a crisp new copy of her novel from out of her tote bag, "and I've decided that it would probably be best to read you a chapter from my book on the history of executions."

"Oh, my," said Alexandra with a worried look on her face. "That does sound interesting."

"Well, don't worry," reassured Glenda in a low conspiratorial tone, "just think, no matter what I've written, it can't be as graphic as what we just saw, right?" Everyone glanced at the bathroom door and gave a chuckle and a self-conscious wince of agreement.

Glenda read to them a brief history of the origins of crucifixion which segued into the popularity of hangings. Her uncomfortable topic was sprinkled delightfully with humorous historical anecdotes of The Doomed and a selection of wry and ironic last words. At times she had to significantly raise her voice to be heard above the group's laughter and the sound of singing and splashing in Moira's tub. To everyone's surprise, in spite of her subject matter, Glenda Guilder was a hit.

After Glenda's reading, everyone got up for a moment to turn the radio back on, stretch, and empty the sangria pot. At this time, the presentation was to be handed over to the three visual artists for their slide show. Brian Epstein had supplied the projector, and so the slides of his sculpture were already in place in the carousel. Ethan and Brandon needed a bit more time to get themselves organized – and Moira was still not out of the tub – so Glenda fiddled a bit more with the fire and Lorna took the opportunity to suggest she and Brian run quickly to the store for more wine and sangria fruit.

They were away for only twenty minutes and by the time they got back, Brandon and Ethan were ready to begin. Moira could still be heard rustling in the bathroom. Lorna rapped on the door and said, "Moira, you're going to prune up in there! We're going to be doing the slides in just a minute."

The splashing got very furious inside for a moment and they heard Moira say, "I'm coming, I'm coming." The gurgle and sucking sound of the drain confirmed her intentions. She emerged soon after that, blood-free, wearing a blue beret like a shower cap and a clean oversized T-shirt.

The evening progressed with demonstrations of sculpture, photography, and paintings, free-flowing wine and the wriest of banter. As the lights were brought back up, all eyes turned to P.J. for he was the only one left to show off.

"So P., whadda you got?" asked Moira. "You bring some poems?"

Everyone echoed her question in similar words, but P.J. just shook his head and looked slightly drunk and uncomfortable. "No. I didn't bring nothing," he said.

"Not nothin' no how?" said Moira, mocking his country accent.

"Nuh uh," he said.

"Do the one about the dog," urged Ethan. "You know that one by heart. You told it to me just yesterday."

"I don't know …"

Voices all around him urged, "Do it. Do it. Oh, come on." Ethan gave him a small push and P.J. stumbled to stand sheepishly by the fireplace. Brandon instantly felt sorry for the boy, but after only a moment's bout of embarrassment, P.J. suddenly calmed himself and seemed to go into a trance-like state. The room hushed. P.J. began.

> "She rises through the roof like smoke.
> No walls can hold, no roof contain,
> The fire of one wrongly wed.
> So to another bed are lain
> The broken vows, pathetic lies
> And when the ceiling cracks above,
> She makes a chimney of her love
> … and flies."

P.J. smiled and shrugged his shoulders as if to say, "That's all folks," and he was greeted with a round of surprised (yet very sincere) applause. Alexandra demanded that he recite one more, but P.J. quickly vacated his moment in the limelight to pour himself another drink.

Ethan rose and put his arm around P.J.'s shoulder. "Good job, old man," he said. "When did you write that one? You see? I knew you could do it." He gave him a warm, manly squeeze and then reached behind him for his coat.

"Where are you going?" asked P.J. with some concern.

"Don't worry about anything," said Ethan. "Everything will be all right."

Alexandra and Brandon were standing close by and heard this last exchange.

"You're not leaving already, are you?" asked Brandon. "Good god, it's only eleven o'clock. The night's still young."

"I have a mountain of work at home," Ethan said.

Alexandra clucked, "But surely it's too late to do any work now."

"'Fraid not," he answered. "I do all my best work in the dark." Ethan waved goodbye to the others in the room and left amid a disappointed chorus of farewell.

"Work, work, work. Is that all you people think about?" said Alexandra to her son.

"Well, obviously I haven't given it a lot of thought myself in the past few days," said Brandon as he sampled quite a healthy dose of P.J.'s bourbon. "What with dead bodies and live mothers cropping up everywhere."

"If I'm too much of a distraction to you, I'll leave."

"You wouldn't dare," chided Brandon. "Not when things are just getting interesting."

"You're right," she agreed.

For the remainder of the party, Lorna led a sing-along at the piano, and Glenda led a vicious gossip attack on the character and actions of Franklin Crown-Smith.

"She doesn't let up on him, does she," said Alexandra privately to Brandon.

"I don't know," he whispered back. "I think you're right, it's just like an adolescent crush. He's all she ever talks about."

"Hmmm," she agreed. "I wonder what her beloved would say if he could hear her now."

As if in answer, the fireplace flue slammed shut with a frightening bang. A dramatic display of sparks and smoke billowed into the room, causing a lot of coughing and a lot of nervous laughter. Lorna wisely got some baking soda and put out the fire, but by that time the room was much too smoky for a party to continue. As it was after midnight, everyone seemed to take the flue's collapse as some sort of prophetic sign, and as a group, decided that it was time to go home.

CHAPTER SIX

Brandon rapped on Ethan's back door. From inside, there was a rustle of newspapers, then a careful pause. Clearly, Ethan was not expecting any visitors at this late hour. It was 1:30 in the morning.

"Yes?" said Ethan's cautious voice.

"'Smee," Brandon said as casually as he could. "Can I come in?"

The sounds of a chair scooting across old linoleum, the pat of bare feet, and the slide of a bolt lock came from within before Ethan opened the door. He was dressed in only a pair of running shorts. Brandon stood there, weaving slightly, and looking more than a little self-conscious. "Is anything wrong?" Ethan asked with concern.

"No," Brandon replied, "I just couldn't sleep, so uh ... I saw your light was on and ..."

"Come on in," Ethan said and reached out a hand to pull Brandon into the room.

Brandon let himself be led into the warm light of Ethan's comfortable old kitchen. From the look of the open newspapers and the open bottle of scotch, he knew he wouldn't have to apologize for interrupting Ethan's work. The air everywhere smelled that peculiar Ethan smell of bay rum and Shower-to-Shower.

"Is the pot luck still going on?"

"Hmm?" said Brandon. "Oh. No, everybody went home." He wasn't sure how well he was hiding the fact that he was slightly drunk from the party. He tried to casually put both his hands in his front pants pockets, then awkwardly realized that that particular act was a very difficult task to do, especially if you and your jeans were just a little bit too tight.

"Come on into the living room," Ethan said. Brandon followed with his hands trapped wrist-deep in denim.

He took a seat on the sofa. Ethan turned on a table lamp, and then went over to the fireplace to light a pressed-wood fire log. The paper wrapper on the manmade log caught quickly and flared up with a flash of purple and green flames. Brandon watched the fire burn and wondered what the hell kind of toxic chemicals they put on those logs to make them blaze so funny.

Ethan offered Brandon a drink, and Brandon accepted even though he suspected he had clearly had too much alcohol already. As Ethan went into the kitchen, Brandon got up off the sofa and freed his hands from their captivity, turning the linings of his pockets inside out as he did so. He quickly shoved the linings back in place and tried to make himself look interested in Ethan's CD player. He pressed play, and the grizzled voice of Tom Waits sang out from the speakers. Feeling appropriately inebriated enough to listen to the odd songs of Tom, Brandon turned the music down low then sat himself on the red industrial carpeting in front of the fireplace.

Ethan came back into the room with two glasses and the bottle of scotch. He handed one of the glasses to Brandon, then joined him in sitting on the floor. "I hope you don't mind me coming over this late," Brandon said. "When I get insomnia like this, I just can't lie around in bed. Usually I get up and watch TV or something, but you know with my Mom here … and no TV, and …"

"Did your Mom go to bed?"

"Yeah," he said, taking a sip from his glass. The liquor burned a little as it went down his throat. "She's sleeping in my living room, so I had to climb out the bedroom window." He smiled and coughed a little from the scotch. Ethan smiled too, and stretched out on the floor. "I tried to discourage Mom from coming here, but she's not one to take anything less than a nuclear weapon as a hint. What are your folks like? Are they still around?"

Ethan stared at the fire. "My Dad's still alive. Up in Montana."

"Does he ever come to visit you?"

"No."

"You're lucky."

Ethan was noncommittal. "I guess," he said.

Brandon sighed and tried not to yawn even though he wanted to. The late hour and the drink made him much sleepier than he pretended to be. The two of them remained silent for a while, listening to Tom Waits and the crackle of the fire. Brandon's mind wandered back to the party and to the strange conversation between P.J. and Ethan. He stretched out on the floor also and propped himself up on one elbow near Ethan's head. "So are you and P.J. pretty good friends, or ..."

"Or what?" asked Ethan, still looking at the fire.

"Or, uh ..." Brandon began to say what he meant, but ended impulsively leaning over and kissing Ethan on the lips. Much to his surprise, Ethan not only kissed back, but kissed back quite well.

They didn't speak again as they continued to softly explore one another right there on the living room carpet. Ethan was deceptively passive at first, letting Brandon take control of their initial fumbling. He allowed Brandon free rein of the soft hairs on his chest and stomach and carefully guided Brandon's curious fingers to places Brandon didn't initially think to go.

Once he felt that Brandon in his inexperience had run out of ideas, Ethan shifted the balance of power and gently took charge. He slipped out of his own shorts then laid Brandon on his back. Ethan slowly peeled Brandon out of his jeans as Brandon undid the buttons on his own shirt. Glad to let the older man do the driving, Brandon tried to breathe deeply and relax. It wasn't easy. Ethan's hungry mouth worked its way from Brandon's armpits and nipples, down to a tender and curious spot in Brandon's inner thighs. The coarseness of Ethan's beard stubble and the warm, wet eagerness of his mouth took a roll call of every inch of Brandon's anatomy, awakening it, defining it, bringing it all into the pulsating present.

Brandon's heart pounded so hard it frightened him. Making love with Ethan was so different from the few strained, awkward collisions he had known in the past. He didn't know what to expect next. He didn't know if there would be some sort of negotiation between them on how far they should dare to go, or if the spoken word was taboo and would break all the delicious tension.

He didn't have long to ponder his immediate future, as Ethan rose and left the room for a moment, retuning with a box of protection. Once Brandon helped him roll on a condom, Ethan reared up and covered Brandon like a hot fur blanket. The sensations that followed were a curious mixture of pleasure and pain that made Brandon stop breathing entirely until he thought he would burst. The long breath he finally let in released something deep down. He felt himself blooming from the inside.

The feeling of Ethan on him and Ethan inside him was just like the warm, rough, tender voice of Tom Waits on the stereo. A masculine growl of sweetness and of sorrow. Brandon prayed that Tom Waits would never stop singing.

They fell asleep together in front of the fire and Brandon dreamed three dreams. The first dream was of a prowling tiger, orange and black and silent, stalking something warm in the night. The second dream was about math class in junior high. The last dream was of a banging drum.

Brandon groaned as he rolled from one side to the other. Would the sound never stop? In his twilight daze, he reached for his pillow to cover his head, to smother his ears, to drown out the pounding of his blossoming hangover. What a headache. And his teeth, well ... he felt as though each tooth wore cashmere. If only that sound would stop. If only the screaming ...

Screaming?

Brandon sat up abruptly and then winced from pain and nausea. Why did he faintly hear the sound of a woman screaming in the distance? And where the hell was he, anyway? Ethan's living room. Ethan's sofa bed. He remembered the first part of the evening but not the last. However, what he realized clearly was that he had to get back to his own bed before Alexandra figured out he had slept somewhere else.

The screams awakened Ethan, also. He got out of bed before Brandon and went to get dressed. Brandon swung his legs slowly over the side of the bed and felt the bite of the morning air on his bare skin. Where were his clothes? Everywhere, it appeared. What was it that he had been drinking? Oh, god. Sangria, Jack Daniels, and scotch. The room spun. Brandon reached to the rough old sofa arm for support and pulled himself slowly into a standing position.

He found his pants and underwear together in a little knot by the living room fireplace. His shirt was tossed under the coffee table. He dressed gingerly, never lowering his head below the level of his shoulders and then padded around the front room in his bare feet until he found his shoes.

Dressed, but bedraggled, he and Ethan both stepped out the front door to see what was the matter. It's funny, he thought, it never occurred to me that it might be Mom screaming. Thankfully, it wasn't. The screams seemed to be coming from the Casa Grande at the end of the drive.

As they passed by Brandon's front door, Alexandra emerged fully dressed, carefully coifed, looking like she had been up for hours. "Where have you been?" she asked with surprise.

"I got up real early and had breakfast with Ethan," he quickly lied. She nodded as though she didn't believe him but was going to accept this explanation anyway. What concerned her more were the sounds coming from the Pembroke house.

Alexandra turned to Ethan and gave a no-nonsense command. "You. Go find a phone and call 911." Ethan complied without a word and started running for the bank of pay phones at the grocery store a few blocks away. "Come on," she said to her son, and Brandon escorted her down the row of cottonwoods to the source of the screams.

The front door of the Casa Grande was wide open. Brandon and Alexandra followed the sound of crying and whimpering inside the house and down the hall. "Hello?" Brandon called out. "Does someone need help?"

"In here," called out a woman's voice. Moira's voice. They walked a little further down the hallway and turned a corner. There, huddled in the door of the Penitente room was Moira cradling a distraught PopIris in her arms.

"What's going on?" asked Brandon as his mother went directly to PopIris' side.

Moira had a comically puzzled, painful look on her face, as though she didn't know quite how to tell him. "It's um, there's uh …" She finally just gave a little nod of her head that instructed Brandon that he should go into the library.

Tentatively, he stepped over the three women stooped in the threshold. At first, the Penitente library looked just like it always did, dark and red and creepy. Out of the corner of his eye, he saw that the rolling library stairs had been knocked over. Turning to face the gargantuan bookcase, he came face to face with the bizarre sight of Franklin Crown-Smith hanging from an iron chandelier hook, his bolo tie as effective as any noose.

Franklin's eyes were open wide and staring at nothing. The tip of his tongue protruded slightly from his lips. More than anything, Brandon thought Franklin appeared to be surprised. The front of Franklin's pants was stained from the moment of death when his bladder relaxed and drained for the final time. The smell of urine mingled in the room with the library's usual scent of juniper and Franklin's own overpowering aftershave.

"Oh, for God's sake," said Alexandra from behind her son.

Brandon turned, startled to see her. "Don't look," he said protectively, and tried to pull his mother away.

Alexandra shrugged him off and continued to stare at the body. "Oh, don't be silly," she said. "You act as if I hadn't seen a man hanged before. Although I admit, Count Guidice looked quite a bit different when we found him hanging from the bell tower. For one thing, he didn't have that ridiculous expression on his face."

How could she make up those stupid stories at a time like this? Brandon backed away from Franklin's body and moved toward the doorway. "Let's get out of here and go call the police," he said.

"They should be here any moment if Ethan did as I asked. I want to take a look around."

"Look around? Mother this is no place for us to be right now."

"Well, we might not get a chance to come back later," she said. "I wonder how it happened."

"How what happened? He committed suicide."

"Well yes," she sighed. "But why are there two pictures missing from that wall?" And it was true. Both the Ansel Adams prints were gone from across the room, their sooty outlines on the white wall marking the spaces where they had once hung. "And the mud," she also observed. "Someone's tracked mud in … through the window." She walked back over to Franklin's suspended body and bent over to see the soles of his shoes. "Wasn't him."

"Wasn't who?" said an oddly familiar Spanish voice. Officer Benitez #45 stood in the doorway watching Alexandra inspect the dead man's shoes.

"Oh, hi," said Brandon, grateful to see the police. "I'm glad you came."

Alexandra backed obediently away as Benitez approached the body. He stared up at Franklin's bug-eyed face, then looked over at Brandon. "What do you do, find one or two dead people a week?" Brandon just gave an embarrassed smile and shrugged. Benitez ushered the two of them out of the room and called for assistance.

Alexandra, Brandon, and Moira sat on the black leather sofa in Franklin's office while they waited for the rest of the authorities to arrive. PopIris had finally collected herself and sat behind Franklin's desk in his high-backed swivel chair, staring blankly out the window into the garden. Alexandra and Moira made small-talk about the party the night before, and Brandon sat silently turning over his own late-night escapades.

The forensics team and coroner arrived accompanied by a host of other uniformed officers. They all secreted themselves back in the library, seeming to take no notice of the four people they were holding in the front office. Brandon could hear the low rumble of male voices in the hallway, but could only speculate on what was actually happening far off in the Penitente

Room. Photos and fingerprints probably, he thought, and that white chalk line around the body. No, wait. You can't draw a chalk line in the air.

His mother was right: the Casa Grande was so solidly constructed a person couldn't possibly hear from the front of the house what was happening in the rear. The only reason they heard the screams that morning was that one library window was wide open. And as for his mother, what was she thinking about? Was she thinking about catching him with Ethan this morning? And where was Ethan now?

One sound that he identified pretty clearly was the clack and rattle of a stretcher bearing Franklin's body down the hallway and out the front door. He glanced over at PopIris to see if she recognized the sound too, but the poor woman continued to stare stoically out the window at two magpies in the fountain.

Brandon was startled out of his thoughts by the sound of Alexandra's voice ringing out. "John!" she called with surprise.

"Hello, Alexandra."

Brandon turned and noticed a man standing in the doorway. Detective John L. Carson stood with his hands in his pockets, turning the room inside out with his eyes. He was a short man with a small build and a face that was attractive in spite of itself. His receding hair and moustache were both black with an even dusting of grey throughout. Unconsciously, he was indulging in his habit of chewing at the corner of his moustache when Alexandra asked, "How long do we have to stay here?"

Detective Carson looked at her with the mildest hint of surprise, then spoke rhetorically. "I don't know," he said. "How long do you want to stay here? Didn't they take your statement already?"

"Who?" asked Alexandra archly.

"Nobody took a statement from you all?" Carson growled in his deep, deep voice that sounded so odd coming out of his little body. "Jesus Christ. Campbell!" he called to a policeman down the hall. "Get in here!" He took out a note pad from his hip pocket and flipped to a blank page. "They're supposed to split you people up and get your statement. I don't know what they think they're up to. Give me the names of everyone who is staying here with the Pembroke."

Moira and Brandon recited the names of all the residents at the Pembroke and PopIris gave her own address in town. PopIris then asked if she might be excused to go lie down in one of the back rooms. Carson gave her leave. Officer Campbell finally came into the office only to receive a stern reprimand from the Detective. Carson then instructed Campbell to get someone to rouse the remaining artists on the grounds. "Ethan Arnold," he said while consulting his notes, "P.J. Copeland and, and ..." He flipped back two pages. "Who else?"

"Glenda," said Brandon. "Glenda Guilder. She's in number seven."

"Guilder in seven," he said, making note of it, "thank you. And the other two, what's their house numbers?"

"Ethan's the first on the road here, number one," said Moira. "And P.J.'s in – what is he in, Brandon? Number six?"

"Six is vacant," said Brandon. "P.J.'s next to it, so that would be number four. Don't forget Lorna and Brian."

"Yes, right," said Carson as he took all this information dutifully down. He then said to the officer, "See if you can get the people in one, four, and seven together for a moment and ... wait a minute." Carson then turned to Moira. "What house are you in?"

"The guest house," she said with a little astonishment. "It's the one right next to the main house. Why?"

"I want you to go with Officer Campbell here and wait until I have a chance to talk with you. Thanks."

Moira looked at Brandon and started to say, "But why can't I ..." but Detective Carson had Officer Campbell remove her quietly from the house. Moira was definitely not happy about the situation, and made that point all too clear; however, she cooperated as best she could.

If Brandon had felt guilty when he ran into his mother after having sex, it was nothing compared to the irrational guilt reflex he was feeling now. Waiting to be interrogated by both the police and his mother was enough to create Guinness-caliber sweat rings. Instantly though, he remembered that Alexandra was not in a position to question him at the moment. Indeed, she was in the same figurative witness box he was. Having her there by his side was suddenly a comfort instead of a terror.

Detective Carson began by looking straight at Brandon and saying, "Looks like you're making a lot of work for us since you rolled into town. A murder on the road, a hanging in the room back there; I hope you're not one of those folks that insists everything happens in threes."

"You don't think I had anything to do with this stuff," Brandon said, with alarm. "I have no idea how Franklin got that way!"

Alexandra patted him on the knee and chuckled. "Calm down, sweetheart. He was joking. No one's accusing you of anything."

"Except being a link," said Carson.

"Well, yes. Except that," agreed Alexandra. "And that is odd, isn't it?"

"It's a coincidence, Mother."

"Maybe," said Detective Carson. "So, tell me a little bit about what happened last night."

"I don't know what happened here last night," said Brandon. "We were all at a pot luck dinner all evening."

"Well, why don't you tell me what happened at the dinner then," said Carson. "What time did you get there?"

"We were early," said Alexandra. "About six thirty."

"And when did you leave?"

Brandon looked at his mother. "I don't know," he said. "Midnight? One?"

"It was closer to one o'clock," said Alexandra. We were there the entire time. Saw everybody come and go. It was a wonderful evening. Food for days and much too much drinking, but it was a party after all and I suppose one does have to let loose once in a while."

"You said you saw everybody come and go. Who else was there the entire time?"

"Well, everybody," said Brandon.

"No," contradicted his mother. "Only Moira was there all the time. Everyone else was in and out all evening."

"Lorna was there all the time," argued Brandon. "She was there when we arrived and ... oh, yeah. She went to the store with Brian."

"At what time?"

Brandon shook his head. "I don't remember."

"Somewhere around ten," said Alexandra. "I remember Ethan left at eleven, because Brandon remarked on it at the time, and the boy ... PeeWee, arrived late. And drunk."

Brandon added, "And Iris wasn't even there at all."

"What about Miss Guilder?"

"Oh, that's right. Glenda didn't leave either once she got there, right Mom? She and Ethan showed up together at, I don't know, 7:30 or thereabouts. Glenda was there all night."

"What time do they think Mr. Crown-Smith died?" asked Alexandra.

"We don't know yet. Could be any time last night," said Detective Carson.

"So, that means all of us could have seen or done something, now doesn't it?" said Alexandra. "It's a good thing that Brandon and I have been together the entire night. At least we can give each other an alibi for the party and all night afterwards. Right, sweetheart?"

Brandon didn't say anything.

CHAPTER SEVEN

"Let's see, what was I going to tell you?" Alexandra let her fork pause halfway to her mouth in thought. "I mean it's all so interesting I know you're just thrilled to hear about the current state of my life. You know, the Alexandra Noble Revised Report. I don't know what it was. I've lost it." She resumed eating and hummed with a mouthful of pleasure at what the chef at Chez Rodriguez had accomplished with green chiles and pate.

She's driving me nuts! said the little voice in Brandon's skull. Run and hide! Call the police! But the truth was, the police were about the last people Brandon wanted to call after having just spent a tedious couple of hours with them being grilled like Labor Day meat.

Well – "grilled," Brandon grudgingly admitted to himself, was probably not the best word for the rather long, informal chat he'd had with Detective Carson and his mother down at the Taos County Court House, but since this was his first murder investigation ever, he preferred to think of himself as having been grilled.

Yes, Frank was indeed dead and it did look like murder, but however unpopular Franklin Crown-Smith seemed to have been among the artists at the Pembroke, Brandon could think of no one among the residents with any reason to kill him. In fact, he'd have supposed that no matter how much they all disliked him personally, it was to everyone's professional advantage to keep

Franklin very much alive. Therefore, since Brandon didn't have much information to give the police, the interrogation turned into something that more resembled a kaffeeklatsch than an interrogation – with Alexandra doing most of the klatsching.

And she was still talking hours later as they ate dinner at one of Taos's tonier restaurants.

"Oh!" she exclaimed. "I was thinking of going to a therapist."

Brandon's fork dropped to his plate with a clatter. The entire restaurant went silent. "Sorry," he said.

"I've decided that you only go around once and since I've been traumatized all my life, it is likely that all of these little skeletons in my closet are going to come out and strangle me to death any day. It could be that this upcoming divorce is the starting of it. But I can't see myself doing it."

"Doing what? Divorce or therapy?"

"Therapy, of course," said Alexandra with surprise. "I have no problems with the divorce. Thornton Noble was a poop. Anyway, I've been giving therapy some thought, but I've decided that it would probably not work."

"Why not?"

"Because," said Alexandra, "I'm more honest than most people and I'm very analytical, and I have a tendency to, to really, what can I say? Oh, I don't know, my mind goes all the time. All I do is think, think, think. And as a result, I probably can tell him all the little intimacies that he would have to pull out of someone else. I would probably tell him, 'And furthermore, this and this and this, and I feel I have a tendency for this, and yes my mother's death traumatized me, and yes I hate men.'"

She paused and looked briefly introspective, an effect that reminded Brandon more of a petit mal seizure than self-realization. "Well certainly not that. I wouldn't say those particular things, just things of that nature, you know. And so the concept that I will talk and solve my own problems just through the realizations of all these wonderfully little 'hidden' things in my life doesn't seem to ring true with me, because, by God, I think I've covered them all."

Brandon let this little revelation ferment a bit while he finished his *Chile vert aux fines herbes* vinaigrette. Dining in a French restaurant in Taos was unsettling enough, what with New Mexicans' propensity to add green chiles to all of the Four Major Food Groups, but hearing his mother admit to doubting her own mental health was too much to swallow. Of course, it was all right for Brandon to think his mother was crazy, but for her to think so of herself, unsettled him deeply.

He reached across the table and took Alexandra's hand. "You'll be okay, Mom," he said. "You always are. Before you know it, you'll be off somewhere, getting married all over again."

"No, I don't think so," she sighed. "Life is just like baseball, you get three strikes … then you're out."

She looked so sad, Brandon had to say something to cheer her up. "But even in baseball," he added, "they always let you have another crack at the bat if you hit something foul."

Alexandra's eyes grew large. "Excuse me?"

"Well, you were the one with the crummy baseball metaphor."

"It wasn't my metaphor. I don't know the first thing about baseball."

"Then why did you say it?"

"I was just repeating what Casey Stengel told me while we were vacationing in the Azores."

Brandon quickly wondered if he could perhaps voluntarily go into a witness relocation program. "Well, the next time you get married, at least warn me about it before I introduce you to any more of my friends. That was so embarrassing."

"You knew perfectly well that I remarried."

"I did not."

"Of course you did," insisted his mother. "You were invited to the wedding. Practically all of North Carolina was."

"North Carolina? I've never been to North Carolina!"

"I know. I was so disappointed you didn't show up. We were expecting you at the plantation. I wanted Thornton to put his elderly mother in your room, but he insisted you would be more comfortable without her in there. The thought of that poor old woman sleeping in the hall on a roll-away bed! I was mortified. But it turned out to be a good thing, you know, what with that fire on the staircase and Winston-Salem going up in flames."

As a young fellow in a ruffly shirt and black velvet vest with the name tag "HELLO MY NAME IS PACO" removed their dinner plates, Brandon decided to steer the conversation into safer waters. "I can't think of anyone who would have wanted to kill Franklin. Can you?"

"Well, no," said Alexandra smoothing out the creases in her napkin, "but then again, I don't know these people and neither do you."

"Of course I do. I've spent every day of the last few weeks with most of them."

"Well, that hardly makes you any sort of expert on anybody. Look at me. I just spent an entire year with a man I assumed was a tobacco sheik. Little did I know that before a year was out I'd be contemplating writing an autobiography titled I Was a Moll for the Ku Klux Klan. Research, my darling, I have found is the key to real peace of mind."

Brandon ordered more sopaipillas and decaffeinated coffee for the two of them, and then inquired, "So you think I should hire a private detective to check out every new friend I meet? Maybe you've got that kind of money, but as for the rest of us …"

"No, I don't mean that at all," said Alexandra taking a fresh, hot bread puff. "Pass the honey, sweetie. Darling. Sugar. Ha ha!

No, I don't mean hire someone to do it at all. I found after being married to Thornton Noble, it's the easiest thing in the world to Goggle anybody."

"You mean Google."

"Certainly. We're in the space age now, or at least we were the last time I looked. They've got records and back issues of everything on the Internet now, all indexed on computers. Fascinating! I did a little snooping online to look up Thornton's family tree for a birthday scrapbook I was putting together for him – and I hot-linked myself right into divorce court. When you start seeing your husband's name next to the sobriquet 'GRAND DRAGON,' you know this marriage cannot be saved."

For the briefest of seconds, Brandon wondered if he should be upset that his mother had turned him into a stepchild of the Klan – then he remembered with relief that she was just making the whole thing up.

Brandon finished his coffee while Alexandra took it upon herself to start a conversation with the elderly tourist couple at the adjoining table. They asked her if she were enjoying her stay. She replied by comparing Taos favorably with all the major capitals of Europe and swore that she would have to tell all her nearest and dearest friends about this charming town; that is, if they ever got a free moment from filming or skiing or ruling the planet.

From the look in the old couple's eyes, it was quite possible that they suspected they had the good fortune to be seated next to some sort of celebrity, although they couldn't quite put their finger on what Alexandra's particular fame might be. Brandon paid the check and got his mother out onto the street before anyone said anything about autographs.

Walking back to the Colony in the dark, they could see the flicker of police lights in front of the artists' cottages. As Brandon and Alexandra got closer, they realized that three police cars were stopped in front of house number one, Ethan's house, and that quite a commotion was happening in his garden.

"You don't suppose they're evicting him for a plant infraction, do you?" mused Alexandra.

"I don't think so," said Brandon, trying not to appear overly alarmed as they approached all the excitement. The blue and white strobes on Ethan's garden set the bushes dancing to the squawk of the shortwave radio and the raised authoritarian voices of young baritone officers. Brandon and Alexandra could only stand mute by the squad cars with the silent group of artists slowly gathering around the scene.

Alexandra, recognizing Officer Campbell of the previous morning, grasped him conspiratorially by the elbow and pulled him close for conference. "Whatever is going on here, Mr. Campbell?" she asked.

Before he had a chance to answer, a brown, muscle-bound policeman came purposefully out of Ethan's house pushing Ethan before him. Ethan appeared to have been caught completely unaware, half dressed, his fringe of hair affright. They thrust him outdoors shoeless and bare-chested, with his hands cuffed behind him.

"Into the car. Watch your head."

Before being forcibly dunked into the back of the squad car, Ethan caught Brandon's eye. The instant conversation they had in a glance surprised him. Brandon expected to see fear or outrage in Ethan's look, but instead, Ethan's dull stare gave no clue as to the inner workings of his mind. No answer to the unasked question on the bitten tongues of each bystander.

"You've got to be joking," said Alexandra (who was never one to bite a tongue) to Officer Campbell. "Tell me you're not doing what it looks like you're doing."

"We got him," said Campbell a little too smugly.

"For what?"

"Burglary and murder. Well, maybe murder," said an unexpectedly deep voice behind them. Brandon and Alexandra turned around quickly and saw that Detective Carson had been standing, small and silent, behind them.

"Murder?" said Alexandra. "Oh really John, don't be silly. What makes you think that poor man is capable of killing anyone?" These were Brandon's very same thoughts, too, but he was glad his mother ended up being the one to voice them. "And what's this about burglary?"

"Alexandra, you know I can't discuss that with you."

That comment pushed a hot button. "Well that's a shame," she said archly. "Especially since I just got you an invitation to visit … um, 'You-know-who.'"

"Hey, are you serious?"

"You asked me, and I said I'd do it. Only now I don't know …"

Detective Carson looked at the policemen guarding Ethan's front door and turned this over in his mind for a second. "When?" he asked.

Alexandra shrugged. "As soon as you can get to Washington. It wasn't easy, let me tell you. And I have to help his wife roll those awful Easter Eggs through the mud next year! It's something I would love to get out of."

Oh, brother! thought Brandon.

Carson motioned with his head toward the front door. "I guess it won't hurt for us to go inside and … have a little talk. You're a key witness in this case, right? Just, uh, don't touch anything." Alexandra gave him a but-of-course look, and Carson led the three of them past the guards into Ethan's living room.

Ethan's dark little house was a disaster inside, a victim of ongoing search warrant vandalism. As Brandon and Alexandra stood by, the police continued in the process of throwing open every cupboard and drawer, scattering hundreds of Ethan's photos and negatives all over the room. They overturned chairs, heaped clothing and papers in piles, and even peeled back the carpeting on one side of the living room exposing the concrete slab beneath. Carson took the Benningtons over to Ethan's sofa which was pulled away from the wall. Behind it were two black and white photographs under glass in gleaming metal frames. Brandon recognized them at once as Franklin's Ansel Adams showpieces from the Penitente room.

"What are these doing here?" asked Brandon.

Alexandra said, "It's rather obvious, dear. Or at least it looks rather obvious." She turned to Carson. "You know someone else could have put these here."

"Someone could have," agreed Detective Carson. "And I considered that, but I found out a lot about your friend here in these past few hours."

Brandon didn't like that sound of that. "Like what?"

"Like, uh, we found out Crown-Smith planned to have Mr. Arnold ejected from the colony soon, and we know that Mr. Arnold loved Ansel Adams, and he's got the shoes that tracked that dirt in from the library window. Three strikes, you're out."

"Baseball has really got a stranglehold on the English language, doesn't it?" mused Alexandra. "I wonder how many more little baseball things we say every day without even thinking? I don't even know anything about the game and I bet I've said he's struck out, or she's been thrown a curve, or … that show's a hit, a million times, and it never even occurred to me until just now that it's all baseball! Isn't that interesting? I remember Casey Stengel said to me …"

"Mother, please."

"What?"

"They just carted my friend off to jail for murder. Casey Stengel has nothing to do with this right now."

"Oh, but he does!" said Alexandra. "I was just taking time to really listen to what we were saying, and besides the fact that America is fixated with baseball, I also noticed that there isn't any evidence that Ethan had anything to do with Franklin's death. Isn't that right, Detective Carson?"

"Technically … yes," agreed Carson. "But it's only a matter of time until we get some answers from forensics and the autopsy."

"And speaking of that, Detective …" said Brandon.

"Yeah?" asked Carson with surprise. "Speaking of what?"

"Speaking of autopsies, did you learn anything about Sienna Sandoval? That woman I found on the Pueblo Road?"

"Yeah, we know all about her. White female, thirty-two, painter from San Diego. Why?"

"Well, I … well, I kind of was curious about how she died because, I guess I'm sort of living in her house now."

Detective Carson gave him a dull, prosaic glare. "We know you're living in her house. What's the problem? You afraid what's happened to her is gonna happen to you?"

Brandon bristled a bit at his tone. "Well, I don't know," he said. "If you tell me what happened to her, then maybe I can decide whether to be nervous or not."

Carson glanced over at Alexandra who stood mutely ravenous for his response. "From what we've gathered," he carefully admitted, "Miss Sandoval was having some sort of relationship with Franklin Crown-Smith. So naturally, we're looking into the possibility that their two deaths are related. Another artist here claims that Sandoval and Crown-Smith were engaged to be married. We haven't found anyone else here who can confirm that. What we can confirm is that they fought a lot."

Brandon gave an exasperated sigh. "So hasn't it occurred to you guys that Franklin killed Sienna, then committed suicide?"

"Did," said Carson. "Did until forensics showed that she was strangled by someone who was prob'ly as tall as Crown-Smith, but was right-handed."

"How could they tell that?" asked Alexandra.

"Oh, they could tell," Brandon admitted, a little deflated that his murder/suicide theory crumbled so quickly. "I saw the strap marks on the back of her neck. They crossed in an X. The left side of the X was pulled up harder and deeper than the right side." He made a couple of fists and crossed his forearms in front of his face as a visual aid. "That means he wrapped the belt around her neck from behind with his right hand, then crossed his right arm up to the left to strangle her. If he were left-handed, it would have been the other way around."

Carson was impressed. "How did you figure that out?"

"I, uh, well, I sit and look at cadavers all day for a living. That's just some of the stuff you pick up, I guess." What Brandon failed to mention was that he once had a brief crush on a young fellow from the police morgue who often made deliveries to Brandon's laboratory. Brandon used to ask him endless questions about forensic science just to keep the gregarious, blond bodybuilder talking. It was a cheap thrill, but as cheap thrills went, at least it was an educational one.

"So Franklin was left-handed," noted Alexandra. She sat on Ethan's sofa and surveyed the wreckage that once was his front room. At her feet was a crumpled photograph of a peony bush in Ethan's little garden. She picked it up and straightened a bent corner. "Well, one good thing," she said, "is you won't try to accuse Ethan Arnold of that poor woman's death. He's certainly tall enough to have done it, but he's left-handed, too."

"Really?" said Brandon. "I never noticed."

"Darling, you never notice anything. He handed you his hoe with his left hand the other day, don't you remember?"

"No."

"And during the slide show, he used his left hand to run the little clicker thing. You know, the thing that makes the slides change."

Carson chuckled softly and looked down at Alexandra on the couch. "You two are good," he said. "We're gonna check out the left-hand thing, though."

"Do that," she said, standing up to leave.

Brandon glanced behind the couch at one of the stolen photographs. A mountain, a moon and a wisp of cloud. Alexandra stood next to him and they both admired it together.

"Well, it is lovely, though, isn't it?" she mused. "But hardly worth killing for."

"Hmm," agreed her son.

She looked up to Detective Carson. "How much would you say these photos are worth?"

Carson pulled a small note pad from his breast pocket and flipped through the pages. "Miss Nelson estimates their value at around five thousand dollars."

"Each?" said Alexandra with surprise.

"I wouldn't think so," said Brandon. "They are Ansel Adams photographs, and they're signed, but they're hardly one-of-a-kind. Look there, that one's numbered. He printed up and signed two hundred and fifty of that one picture alone."

"So, what you're saying," Alexandra incredulously surmised, "is that Mr. Arnold, in a desperate frenzy to have these very affordable photographs, climbed in the window of that awful library, found some way to hoist Franklin to the ceiling by his own necktie, stole these pictures, climbed back out the window again, and then hid the photos behind his own couch."

Carson nodded. "It could happen. Like I said, first of all there was some kind of personality clash between the two. Arnold was breaking some sort of rule you've got here about having a garden or something, so Crown-Smith was getting ready to throw him out. Secondly, we ran a quick check on old Mr. Arnold and found that he'd been arrested three times prior for stealing Ansel Adams photographs from galleries and homes all over the country. He just sees them and he's got to have them. Most times the charges are dropped when he returns the pictures, but once he had to do a month of jail time."

Alexandra looked disappointed. "Dear me," she said. "Well, that doesn't look good, does it."

"No."

Brandon, however, was not disillusioned by this bit of news. "But has he ever been charged with any violent crimes? I just can't imagine Ethan hurting, or even threatening, anybody."

"No," said Detective Carson, "not as far as we can tell. That doesn't mean he could never start, though."

"John, you know perfectly well Ethan Arnold wouldn't hurt a weevil on a corn cob," said Alexandra.

"What?" snorted Brandon.

Alexandra looked a little apologetic. "Well, that's what Thornton would always say, and I thought it sounded so colorful. He said many colorful things, most of which I could never repeat, but weevil on a corn cob was one of his favorites. He also had another one, something about a corn cob in an outhouse but I could never figure out just what it meant. Why a tobacco sheik was fixated on corn I will never know."

CHAPTER EIGHT

The funeral, slow in starting, kept the quiet group of thirty standing half an hour knee-deep in weeds beside the open grave. Surreptitiously bored, Brandon took a deep breath and let his eyes wander from the hole in the ground to the casket beside the hole to the western midday sky turning black in the distance from a gathering thunderstorm. It was a perfect sky for a cemetery, he thought. Not surprisingly for someone with such a ghoulish career, Brandon was a great fan of cemeteries, especially dramatic, disordered cemeteries like this one with lots of character and history.

The cemetery where Franklin was being laid to rest was a colorful jumble of Catholic disorder. White wooden crosses leaned crookedly alongside great marble tombstones, chipped painted plaster statues of the Virgin, and dissolving pale stone tablet grave markers of decades past. Several families had placed ankle-high brick borders around their family plots or had taken the extra precaution of adding a black wrought iron fence to protect their spots. No one planted grass, though. Only un-mown desert grasses, sage and daisies grew at random out of the sticky red earth. These tall, wild graveyard plants overpowered the occasional planned patches of day lilies, small American flags, and sun-bleached plastic bouquets and ribbon work.

In the nearby fields, the meadowlarks noisily defended their territories with twitters echoing in the silence of the air. Brandon looked behind him and admired the green-gray wall of Taos Mountain, dressed also for the funeral in a collar of blackening clouds and a small toupee of snow. Expecting rain, the Rivera Funeral Home had erected a canopy over the sealed casket and draped a large square of Astroturf over the mound of displaced earth. Floral tributes were piled haphazardly under and around the coffin. Someone had even placed the triangle of a neatly folded American flag among the flowers, although no one knew why.

A dozen metal folding chairs were under the canopy, but no one except two older women cared to use them. The women, both overweight and gray, both wearing black dresses and hats, both looking nearsighted and lost, held hands and sat alternately staring at each other, the ground, and the casket. The bronze lettering on the casket lid caught and repelled their glances over and over again: Francisco Juan Albert Corona 1964-2011.

"See, I told you that wasn't really his name," whispered Glenda Guilder to Alexandra. "I wonder whose decision it was to have his real one put on the coffin?"

"Probably the family," said Alexandra.

"You think that's them over there?" asked Brandon with a nod toward the women on the folding chairs.

"Probably," said Brian Epstein, "and good for them. I always thought it was stupid of him changing his name in the first place."

Brandon nodded in agreement, "Death sure pulled him out of the Mexican closet. It's sort of poetic justice, isn't it?"

"A Hispanic in a panic," quipped Glenda. "No, after living most of his life as WASPy Franklin Crown-Smith, poetic justice would have been burying him over there," she said pointing to a nearby shrine made up of a statue of St. Francis standing bemusedly in an upturned blue bathtub. "Anyway, I've seen the headstone. Unfortunately, the name he always preferred will be above ground."

"Well it only makes sense," said Alexandra. "People in the arts are different. You don't see the name Lucille LeSueur on Joan Crawford's grave now, do you?"

"You don't?" asked Brian.

"No," she said, "Christina missed out on a great opportunity."

"Mother," snapped Brandon, "if you even hint that you attended Joan Crawford's funeral, I swear to God I'll have them put Lucille LeSueur on your gravestone."

Alexandra paused and then turned ever so sweetly to Brian. "Never have children, Mr. Epstein," she said. "You give them half your DNA and look at the thanks you get." Brian laughed and then caught himself as he felt the stares of the mourners around him. Alexandra, however, was unabashed. She turned back to her son and said, "Well, if I'm going to go, I'm going to go sitting down. My feet are killing me." She stopped and opened her eyes wide. "Ha!" she laughed, "no pun intended," then walked over to sit with the women on the chairs.

Brandon watched her walk away as Moira, dressed in a scarlet dress, a scarlet hat, and scarlet gloves walked up behind him and slipped her arm in his. "You guys sound like you're having a good time," she said.

"Even at a funeral Mom has to be the center of attention."

"Oh, don't worry about it," said Moira. "It is a funeral, but come on. It's not that solemn an occasion."

"Jesus, Moira, have a heart. You can't actually be enjoying this."

"No one is enjoying the funeral, Brandon," she assured him, "but if you look around, you'll admit this is hardly a grief-stricken crowd."

"You could have at least worn something appropriate," he said.

She adjusted the roses that were askew in her hat and said, "Red was Francisco Juan Albert's favorite color."

Brandon found himself suppressing a smile. "Stop it. This is very serious."

"Oh, very," agreed Moira. "We all loved him so."

"Moira …"

"Loved him to death. So you think Ethan really did it?"

Brandon dislodged himself from her grip. "No! How could you even think such a thing?"

"Well, he was arrested …"

"For stealing some stupid photos!" he said lowing his voice but raising his intensity. "You think he hung a man for a framed print?"

"It's hanged, not hung, me bucko. And then there was the garden," she added.

"Oh, right. So he killed him for petunias."

Moira stopped and looked at Brandon with incredulity. "You mean you didn't know?" she whispered.

"Know what?"

"Ethan," she said with conspiratorial glee, "was growing pot. He had the biggest crop in the whole town."

Brandon was stunned. "Where?!"

Moira eyes gleamed as she drew Brandon closer. "He has like this gift for gardening, Brando. He planted marijuana among the poppies … cute, huh? … and then trimmed all the leaves back so it looked like some other kind of bush. Then he'd dry and sell the clippings. He's a genius."

"How do you know all this?"

Moira stepped back and shook her head. "Oh, Brandon," she said, "who do you think he sold the clippings to?" She smiled and glided serenely into the crowd.

Brandon couldn't quite believe Moira's revelation at first, but at the same time, he couldn't quite disbelieve it, either. Actually, growing marijuana in the garden would account for quite a lot of Ethan's eccentricities. Brandon always thought it was strange that Ethan insisted on working after the hour of midnight, and he thought it was even stranger that he would save his bath and kitchen drainage to water his precious little plants. It would also explain Glenda's report that Franklin was irate about the garden. Somehow Franklin must have found out what Ethan was doing, and must have been determined to stop it before the whole community found out about it, too.

Brandon looked over at PopIris, standing stiff and cold on the other side of the coffin. Did she tell Franklin what Ethan was growing? How did she find out? Did Glenda tell her? Ethan probably had quite a lucrative little income from his plot and was loath to see it end. But was it all worth killing for?

No, it was not worth killing for. Ethan was innocent – and Brandon was the only one who could be certain of it.

A sick feeling rolled across the pit of his stomach every time he thought about Ethan sitting in jail. Although he didn't want to admit it, guilt was eating him up from the inside. Ethan was in jail and all it would take was one word from Brandon to free him. He could picture it now, marching up to the jail and announcing, 'Hello, I'm Brandon Bennington and I say Ethan Arnold couldn't have killed Franklin Crown-Smith! He was with me all night. I was his lover!'

Could he bring himself to do that? No, he couldn't. He was just too afraid. Too big a closet case. Still, if it looked like Ethan were actually going to be convicted (or executed!), he'd have no choice but to tell the world 'He's innocent because I'm a big old queer.' Ack! But if Ethan were proved innocent some other way...

That's it. Brandon would find some other way to get Ethan out of jail. If he could tell the police who really killed Franklin, they would have to let Ethan go.

But how could he find this out?

His mother, of course. Alexandra had found out the awful truth about her last husband, and even if her conclusions were overblown dramatic fiction, her research methods seemed solid enough. Yes, he would ask his mother for help.

He spotted her on the folding chairs talking with the two heavy-set women. Alexandra wasn't saying much, only nodding sympathetically and listening intently to what appeared to be quite a load of stories. One woman, the larger of the two who looked to be about sixty, spoke rapidly and used the wave of her handkerchief often and for effect. She was a pleasant looking lady, more Mexican-American in dress and in manner than in physiognomy. Brandon could tell when Alexandra was complimenting her on her hat or on her dress, because the hand with the handkerchief would float to the item of note, adjust it, or smooth it self-consciously. A sad and grateful smile would appear on her face and the stories would tumble from her faster than before.

The other woman was much older and quieter. Although just as plump as her companion, she was a small individual with little brown features and thin white hair. She sat obediently at the side of the larger woman and stayed out of the conversation altogether.

As Brandon approached them, he heard his mother say, "Oh! This is my son, Brandon. Brandon, come over here and say hello, won't you?" He stood beside Alexandra, and nodded politely to the two women. He was careful not to smile, since after all, he was at a funeral and these could possibly be the only two bereaved.

"Hello," he said.

"Brandon, I'd like you to meet Mrs. Corona." She touched the large, well-dressed woman with the handkerchief on the hand. "She's Franklin's mother, and this is a friend of the family, Mrs. ... Mrs. oh, dear ..."

"This is Matilda Chimoro," said Franklin's mother gesturing to the smaller, older woman.

"I am so sorry, Matilda. Please forgive me," said Alexandra. "Matilda also knew Franklin as a little boy. She helped to raise him, in fact. What were you, Matilda? A governess?"

"Oh, no," said Mrs. Corona.

"Oh, no," echoed Matilda with surprise and humility. "I was just the housekeeper. Marlene, she take care of the baby."

"But Matilda was a great help," added Mrs. Corona with a handkerchief pat on Matilda's hands. "I don't know what I could have done without her."

Alexandra turned to Brandon and said, "It turns out that Mrs. Corona ..."

"Marlene," insisted Mrs. Corona.

"... Marlene is originally from Denver, and I mentioned to her that I had spent some considerable time in Denver and it just so happens that she is actually related to the Washburns, Mr. Peters's cousins' best friends. I spent an entire winter skiing with them in the Rockies, you know, the year the Pope came through!"

"Ai!" exclaimed Matilda. "Did you see him?"

"Oh, of course," began Alexandra, but Brandon cut her off.

"I'm very sorry about Franklin, uh, Francisco," he said.

"Ai!" said Matilda, who hung her head.

"Thank you, so much," said Mrs. Corona. "We're still in such a state of shock. I understand you were a writer at the colony."

"A painter," corrected Brandon, "and I'm still there. At least I think I am. I have no idea what's going to happen now that

Franklin's gone. It's funny, but I haven't even thought about it until just this second."

"I'm sure the colony will go on," said Mrs. Corona. "That is what Frankie would have wanted. I'm sure they made some provisions in case something should happen to him."

"Ai! The monster!" exclaimed Matilda.

"Excuse me?" said Alexandra.

Marlene Corona put a sympathetic arm around Matilda and explained to Brandon and Alexandra, "Matilda was very close to little Frankie. Don't worry dear," she said to her companion, "they've got him in jail. The law will take care of him."

"They should hang him slowly then shoot him with a thousand bullets," said Matilda bitterly.

The image of Matilda Chimoro taking pot shots at Ethan Arnold's dangling body immediately appeared before Brandon. "We have to be sure they accuse the right person, though," he said quickly.

"Well, yes," said Mrs. Corona with one knitted brow. "The police know what they're doing. I'm sure we should leave it to them."

"The monster!" wailed Matilda again and Marlene Corona comforted her.

Everyone quieted and came to attention as the service at the grave side started. Alexandra took Brandon by the hand and led him to the opposite side of the canopy where they could better hear the words of the minister.

"Episcopal," whispered Glenda Guilder from behind them. "Wouldn't you know it?"

Afterwards, as they were walking to the plaza, Brandon asked his mother what her immediate plans were. "I thought I'd be off soon," she said. "I thought maybe I'd drive around and see the area for a few days. After all, I've got the use of the rental car for another whole week and you haven't let me use it once since I've been here. I've never done so much walking in my life."

"I thought you were the one who climbed an alp."

"I mean, my God, I climbed an alp, but I certainly didn't walk this far."

Brandon stopped and looked in an art gallery window and stared at a lithograph by Armado Peña. "I was wondering if maybe you might drive me to the library tomorrow morning," he said.

"Drive? To the library? Why? Where is it?"

"It's just a few blocks away. It's not far."

Alexandra paused. She looked at Brandon. She looked at the Peña print. She looked back at Brandon. "What is it you really want?"

"Nothing. Why do you ask?"

"Because I have a sneaking suspicion that you aren't totally convinced that your friend Ethan is completely guilty or completely innocent and that you want to do a little research and see if you can find out anything on him."

"What makes you think that?"

"Because you're the world's worst actor and I can read you like a thermometer. If you want some advice, why don't you just ask for it?"

Brandon sighed and said, "All right, Mother. Will you go with me to the library and show me on their computers what you had to do to find out all that stuff about your last husband?"

"No," she said.

"No?"

"You obviously have no idea what you're doing, Brandon. The most logical first place to check if you want to learn about any of your Colony friends is right under your nose."

Brandon thought a moment, and then shook his head in exasperation. "I don't know," he said. "Where do I look?"

"Think," she insisted.

"Well … if I wanted to find out about someone at the Pembroke, I would look …" He looked in the window at the Peña print again. It was a graphic of a Pueblo woman standing in front of a blue door. It was titled "Home." "Home," he said, "I would look at the Pembroke."

"Precisely! I was beginning to wonder if you had half my DNA after all. The place for you to look is in the files in Franklin's office."

"Oh yeah, right," snorted Brandon. "And like how am I supposed to do that?"

"Steal them!" Alexandra said with just too much of an excited gleam in her eye.

"Oh, Mother. Really."

"I'm serious. Well, you don't need to steal them permanently you know. All you have to do is borrow them for a few hours. And while you're at it, get everybody's file. You might as well see what you can find out about the whole crew."

"But why?" he asked.

"Because if you're going to try to discredit Detective Carson's theory, you might have a better chance of convincing him if you give him one or two new theories to pursue."

"So to help Ethan, you're suggesting that I turn in all my other friends?"

"No," said Alexandra. "Not if they're innocent. Besides, it'll be fun looking at everyone's files, don't you think?"

Against his better judgment, Brandon allowed Alexandra to map out a strategy for obtaining the Pembroke residents' personal files. Her mind worked in such a blaze of speed and accuracy that Brandon suspected she had been planning for such an event from the moment she arrived in Taos.

Basically, her plan was to take PopIris Nelson out to lunch, and have Brandon lift the paperwork while they were gone. It seemed simple enough. Ordinarily, the introverted and studious Iris would not socialize at all, but Alexandra was confident enough in her own persuasive abilities to get PopIris to agree to go. The hard part was to cleave PopIris from her keys to both the front door and files before they left for the restaurant.

As it turned out, PopIris did not want to be alone on the afternoon following the funeral, so she accepted Alexandra's invitation a little bit too quickly and a little bit too desperately. Apparently, the woman needed a lunch.

Alexandra was careful to note that PopIris had only one purse. It was black and very simple with a long shoulder strap. Since shopping in Taos offered very limited choices, it only took three tries before she happened upon the discount department store on Paseo del Pueblo Sur which had a dozen purses for sale identical to the one PopIris had. ("I can't believe I'm reduced to buying an eight-dollar purse!" she remarked to Brandon later.)

She called on PopIris at the Casa Grande at 2:00.

True to form, PopIris Nelson was sitting in a chair in the front hall of the Casa, her black Dutch boy combed, her black purse in her lap, and her black eye staring into space, ready and willing to go the minute Alexandra should come to call on her. She did not even invite Alexandra inside after she answered the bell, but rather stepped outside and locked the door behind her the moment after hello.

Brandon came running up, out of breath up the drive. In his arms, he carried a large armload of thick art books. "Mother! Wait!" he cried.

"Oh, what is it now," said Alexandra impatiently.

"While you're out, could you return all these books to the library for me? You know, since you've got the car and all, it'll save me from lugging them all back over there on foot."

"Well, all right," she sighed. "Just put them in the … oh, wait. Brandon, dear could you loan me twenty dollars? I was going to go to the bank before lunch, but if you could see me clear, I can go tomorrow and pay you back."

"Well," he said, "I don't know. I'll have to see what I've got on me. Here Iris, could you hold these a minute?" And with that, he unloaded his unwieldy stack into PopIris' unwelcoming arms. Alexandra held PopIris' purse, while Brandon looked into his wallet and slowly counted out twenty one-dollar bills and handed them to his mother. "You know, this cleans me out, Mom."

"I'll pay you back tomorrow. I promise."

PopIris moaned. "These are awfully heavy."

"Oh, I'm sorry!" said Brandon. "Here, let me put them in the back seat of the car. Thanks for returning these, Mom. Remember, they've got to go back today, or I'll have to pay an overdue fine."

"All right, all right. I'll remember. Iris, here's your purse."

PopIris took the purse and straightened her clothing. "Thank you," she said and climbed into the car. She never noticed that Alexandra switched the handbags and she never paid any attention when Alexandra opened up the black purse she was currently holding and casually handed a set of keys to her son before giving him a quick kiss goodbye.

Brandon waved to the rental car as it headed down the dusty drive for what was promised to be a very long afternoon. He looked casually around and after assuring himself that no one was watching, he let himself in the front door of the Casa Grande.

He nipped quickly through the darkened adobe foyer to Franklin's office on the north side of the building. There were four filing cabinets in the room and two drawers of files in his massive mahogany desk. Where to start? The drawers of all the filing cabinets were labeled in PopIris's anal block handwriting. It took a quick scan of the categories to guess that the papers he was most interested in were probably in the desk.

Like a real professional burglar, Brandon thought ahead and brought a pair of rubber dishwashing gloves to wear while doing the heist. They actually made him look more like a cleaning lady than a thief, but at least he wouldn't leave any fingerprints. The smallest key on the ring fit the lock above the pencil drawer and Brandon slid the left-hand file open first. Financial reports, grant applications, tax forms and an extra box of file folders were all that met his glance. It was in the right-hand drawer that he struck pay dirt.

In alphabetical order were the individual files of the seven artists in residence. Behind them were the dossiers of the artists due to come later in the season. Out of sheer curiosity, Brandon pulled his own folder first and looked inside. On top was, of course, his application and the plastic sheet of photographic slides. The bad, double-exposed ones. He winced at the trite essay question answers that he gave and double-winced at the photo booth portrait he submitted as a picture of himself. Attached with a paper clip was a one page handwritten evaluation of Brandon's talents. It was Franklin's writing.

"… Lacks spontaneity, imagination and fluidity of strokes … Great skill in handling detail. Nightmarish images of duality of realism interesting but unconvincing … Shows promise." Jerk. A little cryptic note from PopIris noting Brandon's time of arrival was penned on the corner of the evaluation in her boxy little handwriting.

Disgusted, Brandon slammed the folder shut and reached for Ethan's file. An eight by ten, black-and-white self-portrait was on top. The skill of Ethan Arnold the photographer caught the personality of Ethan Arnold the subject in the deeply shadowed study he had done of himself. His expression was an odd combination of contrasts: distant yet friendly, unsmiling yet beatific. After a quick scan of the rest of the file's contents Brandon found nothing very enlightening, except PopIris's note "prev 2010 res," but perhaps his mother would see something he was missing.

As he gathered up all the files into a neat stack, Brandon peeked quickly at Moira's folder. "Moira Atchison, 314 West 45th Street, New York, New York," it read. She didn't tell me she lived in Hell's Kitchen, he mused. Next to her application was her black-and-white portrait. PopIris had doodled "fri630" in the corner. Moira's photo was one of those actor's head shots that get reproduced by the hundreds, and true to form, it didn't look much like her. Her hair was very different when she had the picture taken and with makeup and airbrushing, the only recognizable part of her face was the crinkle of her eyes. Brandon was disappointed. He would have thought Moira of all people would not have stooped to marketing herself in such a pedestrian, glamour-gal fashion. Apparently, his mother was right. Perhaps he didn't know these people as well as he liked to imagine.

Time was racing. Alexandra promised that she would keep PopIris away from the Casa Grande until at least 4:00, but even she couldn't work miracles. He had a lot of work to do. He gathered up all seven folders under his arm, closed the drawers, locked the desk and slipped out the front door of the house.

Now, he thought, let's pray that the photocopy machine at the drug store is working.

CHAPTER NINE

Franklin Crown-Smith was forty-seven years old at the time of his death. Even though Franklin's roots were not in Taos, the local paper painted him as a shining, dead example of a successful hometown boy. As the founder of Opera West! in New York and Director of the Pembroke Colony for the Arts in Taos, he was just notable enough to receive obituary notices in all the major south-western dailies as well as brief notices in The Denver Post and The New York Times.

Alexandra had a stack of these newspapers and the photocopies of the Pembroke files on her lap as she sat on the passenger side of the little brown rental car. With the glasses she never wore in public teetering on the tip of her nose, she read aloud the most interesting newspaper accounts to Brandon who kept his attention mostly between his very bad driving and the road map draped precariously on the dash.

The brown scrubby desert around Tres Piedras gave way abruptly to the lush mountain greenery of the Carson National Forest. When he agreed to drive his mother to Farmington, New Mexico, Brandon had never imagined that the flat, straight roads that surrounded Taos would suddenly turn to alpine hairpins. He was never comfortable driving anywhere, so the change in scenery was more than upsetting to him. Alexandra, however, was oblivious to the variety of New Mexican terrain.

"Are these the best photocopies you could make, darling?" she asked in her most imperious tone.

"What do you want?" he snapped while rounding an uphill turn a little too tightly. "I'm in a goddamn drugstore with bright yellow rubber gloves on photocopying stolen files and trying not to look conspicuous. I wasn't really worrying about the quality of the prints I was making."

"Well they're much too faint. I prefer copies with a higher contrast."

"I'll remember that on our next heist … Jesus!"

"What's the matter? Darling, you're driving much too close to the edge of this cliff here."

Brandon gripped the steering wheel tighter and continued his precarious climb along the twisting forest road. The radio sputtered and popped as they lost the faint signal through the mountains. Brandon briefly tried tuning in to a stronger station, but his tenuous driving suffered greatly. He quickly gave up and snapped off the radio with an impatient flick of his wrist. Alexandra sat and hummed the last heard pop song fragment as she shuffled through her papers.

"You see, I knew it."

"You knew what, Mother?"

"GooGoo L'Amour is thirty-seven years old."

"You're kidding. I had no idea."

"A woman can always tell another woman's age. One hundred percent of the time. Sometimes. Oh, look at that gorgeous view! You can see thousands of feet straight down! Try not to take the curves quite so tightly, would you dear? Thank you. Well, this is odd."

"What's odd?"

"On her application, she wrote 'In case of emergency, contact whoever the hell gives a shit.' Hmmm. I wonder why she wrote that?"

"What are you worried about, her bad grammar or the fact she doesn't have any relatives? Her parents are dead."

"Oh, really? And she didn't have any brothers or sisters?"

"Yeah, she said she had a sister named Maria who died, too."

"That's too bad. How'd she die?"

"I don't know. Moira didn't say."

Alexandra flipped through a few more pages. "Let's see now, Peter James Copeland, blah blah blah, retarded genius, blah blah blah … Lorna Shaw … lovely girl. Oh, that's right, Ethan did say that Lorna had been here last year, too. Apparently without her boyfriend. Well, listen to this! It says here she's performed at Carnegie Hall! Oh, Carnegie Recital Hall. Well, that's different."

"You are such a snob."

"No I'm not. I just don't believe in dropping names."

"You drop names all the time!"

"Not second-rate names." Alexandra glanced back out the car window again. "Well now, there's another one. I've been meaning to ask you something, Brandon, ever since I've come to New Mexico."

"What is that?"

"You see those white crosses by the roadside? See right up there? There's five of them right there in a bunch and one a bit further down. What exactly are those for?"

The car swerved nauseatingly along a double downhill hairpin as white cross after white cross flashed by. "That's where someone was killed in a car wreck," he said. "One cross for each dead body. They're supposed to remind you to be a little more cautious. Works for me."

"Oh dear," she sighed. "It does give one pause. I wonder if they have little pictures of wedding bells and fetuses posted up on Lover's Lane."

"I doubt it," he said.

"Which reminds me of the other topic I've been meaning to ask you about, darling."

"What's that?"

"Romance. I haven't any idea who you're seeing or how you're doing in that department."

Brandon gripped the steering wheel tighter. "Mother, we don't want to have that conversation right now."

Alexandra paused and counted two more white crosses. "We don't?"

"No," he said.

"Oh."

Brandon looked over at her. His mother could pack a vowel with more subtext than any woman he knew. "What do you mean, 'Oh?'"

"Nothing. What do you mean?"

"Nothing."

"Oh."

They sat in silence as the forest returned to desert. A sign appeared informing them they were finally leaving the Carson National Forest.

"Only one hundred more miles to Farmington," Brandon said.

Marlene Corona's knees pressed her blue plastic kneeling pad inextricably into the dirt as she weeded the flower beds in front of her house. She pushed back the brim of her sun hat and stared with amazement as she saw Brandon and Alexandra's car pull into her driveway. At first it was obvious that she did not have a clue whom her visitors were, but as soon as Alexandra stepped out of the car and waved, Marlene's face brightened and she struggled to her feet, leaving her kneeling pad and trowel right where they lay.

Alexandra walked over to Marlene and gave her a long hug. Although they had only met two days earlier, Franklin's mother welcomed Alexandra as warmly to her home as she would have welcomed her oldest and dearest friend. Brandon, feeling more than a little uncomfortable with the situation, lingered in the car a bit longer on the pretext of refolding road maps and straightening Alexandra's paper piles of evidence. He was finally coaxed out of the car by the insistent waving and squealing of the two ebullient mothers.

The Corona family home was a large 'fifties split-level painted a demure drunken white trimmed in a fairly sobering shade of cow teat pink. Although it was basically just an overblown suburban tract-house, in the context of the neighborhood it seemed more like a mansion, its large asphalt gables looming imposingly over the more traditional New Mexican adobes and aluminum mobile homes adjacent. In a town in which almost every home had a car chassis on cinder blocks as a lawn ornament, the Corona's green grass and weeping willow seemed rather elegant in comparison.

It appeared to Brandon that Marlene Corona went to extraordinary lengths to resemble her house, too. Along with her monumental bulk, her floppy pink gardening hat perfectly matched her gardening gloves and pink synthetic slacks – slacks that remained spotless even with all the kneeling and digging she had apparently been doing for hours. Also, like her slacks, her white tunic-style blouse remained inexplicably unsoiled and crisp.

Alexandra took a moment to compliment Marlene on her roses and lobelia, which Brandon also had to admit were spectacular. The garden made him think about Ethan, though, and how much Ethan would enjoy seeing the flower beds, too – but then again, maybe he would not, since this was the garden of the mother of the man he was accused of killing.

"I had no idea you two would be in Farmington so soon," said Marlene.

"Well, as a matter of fact, Marlene," replied Alexandra, "neither did I. It was only yesterday – wasn't it Brandon? – yesterday that I suddenly realized that I only have one week left of my trip to New Mexico and all that I've really seen is Taos. I read about this wonderful thing you have out here called the shipstone …"

"Shiprock, Mother," corrected Brandon.

"Shiprock, yes, well anyway I saw it on a postcard and knew I had to see it in person before I go. I had no idea that the drive would be quite so far. It doesn't look that far on the map, but one thing I noticed right away was that this little trip would take us right through Farmington. So here we are."

"Come on inside," said Marlene. "Matilda Chimoro was just about to start dinner. I'll have her add two more places."

"Thank you," said Brandon.

Alexandra laid a firm hand on her son's forearm and protested. "Oh no, we couldn't impose. We were just passing through on our way to Shipstone and thought we'd say hello."

Now Brandon knew very well that they had no intention of seeing Shiprock and that the only reason they came to Farmington was to pump Marlene Corona for information about Franklin, but what finesse his mother had! Left to his own devices, Brandon would probably have marched right up to Mrs. Corona and started firing questions at her. Questions she would probably refrain from answering.

Alexandra's approach definitely appeared to be the preferred method of investigation in this situation. If they let the unsuspecting woman just chatter on under the guise of casual conversation, they could be assured of a wealth of disclosures, because with Alexandra Bennington Peters (et. al.) as her conversational competitor, Marlene Corona would be certain to spill big beans just to keep up.

"I insist that you stay for dinner," said Marlene.

"Well if you're sure it isn't too much trouble …"

"Nonsense! Matilda Chimoro would be delighted to have company. She's a tremendous cook and a shameless show-off in the kitchen. I'm sure she'll jump at the chance to have fresh victims."

And so will my mother, thought Brandon.

As it turned out, Matilda Chimoro was indeed thrilled at the chance to get cooking on all four burners for the Benningtons. During a quick guided tour of the house, Alexandra kept remarking on what a spotless housekeeper Matilda was and how fortunate Marlene Corona must feel to have such a treasure as both an employee and trusted companion. Both women took all of this in and fairly combusted with pride. After that, there was nothing they would not show Alexandra. Upon retiring to the living room, Marlene and Matilda both went directly for the family albums and laid them casually on the coffee table in front of Alexandra. Here we go, thought Brandon, but Alexandra did not pick up the albums right away. First she settled back and complimented Marlene on her decorating taste in furnishing the room they were sitting in.

Now, a compliment like that would never have occurred to Brandon, since he found the decor of the entire house to be uncomfortably a little bit too Middle American, a cloying, artificial style he particularly disliked. But Alexandra knew what she was doing.

"This room has very much the same feeling that the villa had when I stayed at that charming place in the Loire valley. Such warmth and good clean lines. Perhaps you know of it. Have you ever been to France?"

Marlene Corona's eyes widened, and then drooped a little at the corners with sadness. "Well yes, but only to Paris. We were there, you know, for Frankie's debut at the Paris Opera." She wiped away a little tear with a tissue from her pocket before apologizing for getting emotional. "I keep forgetting that he's gone," she said.

"I understand," nodded Alexandra.

Brandon, uncomfortable with the sudden funereal turn the conversation had just taken, tried to lighten things up a bit. "I've never been to France at all," he said.

"Yes, that's true," Alexandra added, following his lead, "although I've begged him to travel with me every time I go abroad."

"You have?" he snorted, and his mother shot him such a subtle and ferocious glance that he sputtered "I mean, you have. I never can seem to get away."

"I have pictures of the opening in Paris right here if you'd like to see them," said Marlene.

"That would be wonderful!" Alexandra gurgled and scooted over on the plump floral sofa so Marlene could sit beside her and narrate. "These are just some high school pictures of Frankie. Oh! Here he is after his first recital at the Civic Center."

Alexandra peered carefully at the photograph. "Well, it looks like he was popular with the girls. They're hanging all over him."

Marlene nodded. "Yes, um, those are a couple of Matilda's kids and that's poor Peggy Martinez. Poor thing was killed only a few weeks after that picture was taken. Somebody choked the life right out of her. They never caught him. Frankie was so upset." She abruptly turned the page. "We don't talk about that much. Here's Frankie after he graduated, 1983, I think. The year he went off to New York."

Since he couldn't see the album from where he was sitting, Brandon started to feel a little left out. "What did Mr. Corona do for a living?" he asked.

"My husband? We owned a large company," she replied absently. "Baked goods."

"Well, whatever Matilda is baking in the kitchen smells great," he said. "You think she'd mind if I went to snoop on her?"

"She'd love it, but don't be disappointed if she doesn't talk much. Matilda Chimoro is a quiet one."

"So am I," he replied and arose to seek out the kitchen.

Brandon crossed through the dining room and found the kitchen logically attached. Matilda Chimoro was bent over a cutting board on the counter in one corner, surgically dissecting a stack of mild green chiles. Brandon said hello and she looked up first with a start and then with a smile.

"I had to come in here and see what you were doing," he said. "It smells wonderful."

Matilda shyly tittered and said thank you while she continued her surgery. Brandon lifted the lid on a simmering pot on the stove and was blasted with a face full of pungent steam. "My god! This looks amazing. What are you making?"

"Posole," she said.

Brandon took a moment to think. "Po-so-lay," he said. "Okay ... so what are you making?"

Matilda smiled and took the lid from his hand and replaced it on the pot. "It's like a stew," she said, "with hominy and pork. Marlene, she don't know I'm making it tonight, so don't you tell her till it's on the table."

"Why's it a secret?" he asked.

"She don't want me to cook Espanish no more. Not since her husband, Sr. Corona died."

"That's odd."

Matilda Chimoro shrugged. "She's not Espanish. She's some other kind of white so she likes things more American than it was when her husband was alive."

"She told us that they had their own baked goods business," he said.

"Is that what she said?" mused Matilda.

"Uh huh," he replied. "Does she still run it?"

"They sold it maybe ten years ago to a big company for lots of money. They cooked tortillas."

Brandon stayed in the kitchen with Matilda Chimoro for the next half hour as she cooked and talked with gathering momentum until he fairly couldn't shut her up. Apparently, thought Brandon, Mrs. Corona considered Matilda to be tight-lipped only because she never took the time to listen to her. With a willing and captive audience, Matilda Chimoro rolled a long and twisted history of the Coronas as she rolled two dozen tortillas for dinner.

"Frankie's father, Señor Corona, he was a big man. Very big. Tall as the door and three hundred pounds. He met the Señora when he was in the navy. It was in San Diego and I think she was going to have a baby, so her family was very upset 'cause she was white. Very bad. After the war they come back here to Farmington 'cause his mother she makes tortillas and he sells them to the stores in the neighborhood. One day Señor Corona he sells the tortillas to the biggest restaurant in town and they make a little money. So he sees he can make more money if his mother she makes more tortillas ... but she's old, so he gets Marlene to learn to make the tortillas and she wanted no part of it. But Señor Corona, he's a drinker and he breaks her ribs in a fight so she cooks the tortillas whether she wants to or not."

"He broke her ribs?" interrupted Brandon with astonishment.

Matilda Chimoro looked at him blankly and said yes like it was the most natural thing in the world. "When he was drunk, he was mad. Back in those days she always had a bruise somewhere. Many women did, but we did not talk about it. I came to the family when they started selling many tortillas and Marlene had no time to take care of the house."

"So how long did all this keep up? I can't really picture Mrs. Corona cooking tortillas for very long."

"I don't know," said Matilda Chimoro. "Ten years, I guess."

"Ten years?" he sputtered. "She made tortillas with her mother-in-law for ten years?"

Matilda laughed. "The Señor's mother she died pretty soon. They got a real big kitchen and hired some more people. Then they got rich."

Well, rich for Farmington, Brandon noted to himself. "What did Franklin do during all this time? Did they make him help out in the business?" he asked aloud.

"No, he was their angel," she said as the ladled posole into a glazed terra cotta tureen. "Francisco was raised like a child of the money. He never knew them when they lived in the small house with Old Lady Corona or when his mother sat in abuela's kitchen with the tortillas. By the time he started in school, they had the factory."

"Tell me some more about his father's drinking."

"Why do you want to know?" she asked as she layered a serving tray with dinner plates, napkins and silverware.

"My Dad was an alcoholic, too," Brandon lied. My mother will kill me when she hears this, he thought.

"He was a good man," said Matilda Chimoro. "I don't want to say bad things about him. He was a good man."

"A good man who beat his wife."

"A wife should do what her husband says and not keep him awake all night complaining that the house is too small or his English is too bad. A wife should not be embarrassed by her husband even if he is not white."

Noting the bitterness in her voice, Brandon took the tray from her and said, "I thought that you two were supposed to be very close friends."

Matilda hoisted the tureen of posole and looked Brandon straight in the eye. "We are friends. We are friends because we were both close to Frankie." She paused and walked to the kitchen door with her load. Brandon followed with the tray. "But Frankie is dead now," she said and their discussion was ended, and they set the table together in the dining room.

The evening meal proceeded congenially enough. Alexandra entertained with leading anecdotes of her life and times culled from her vast (and largely apocryphal) history. Her stories were meant to pull similar anecdotal nuggets from Matilda and Marlene, but it soon became evident to Brandon and Alexandra that as long as the other one was within earshot, Marlene and Matilda kept their views to themselves.

Through silent glances and a discrete raised eyebrow over dessert, Brandon knew that his mother wanted to leave right after dinner so she could find out what Matilda Chimoro said in the kitchen. As he was just as eager for escape, they embarrassingly both made their exit apologies simultaneously to Marlene Corona, who laughed and said she understood perfectly as it was definitely getting late and Shiprock was still another forty-five minute drive away.

"You will be coming back through Farmington again, won't you?" asked Marlene.

"I go everywhere," stated Alexandra. "Isn't that right, Brandon? I go everywhere and you'll never know when I'll turn up."

"Yeah, it's true, Mrs. Corona," said Brandon. "After you've known my mother for a while, you'll start checking behind the shower curtain whenever you go to wash your face."

Alexandra slung her purse dramatically over her shoulder and said, "I surprised him once in a men's room when he was in junior high and he's never forgiven me since."

"It was a locker room – in college – and I've completely repressed every single embarrassing detail."

"So be on guard," said Alexandra to Marlene, "and don't take up a dangerous sport like ice hockey or I'll burst in on you, too."

Mrs. Corona did not know how to follow this seeming non sequitur and sputtered something like "It's hardly likely" and Brandon bit the inside of his cheek to keep from laughing. He could tell Marlene was conjuring the image of her round little matronly self going for a slap-shot on the ice.

They got in the car and drove off in exactly the wrong direction to Shiprock. "I suppose I should have at least made the pretence of going where we said we were," observed Brandon a few blocks later, "but I completely forgot all about it back there."

"So did I," admitted Alexandra. "And that is precisely the problem with lies. You keep forgetting your story. In the same token, it's also why lies are so easy to figure out in others."

"So what did you find out?"

"I'm tired," she said as they drove down the wide Farmington business strip. "Let's find a room so I can collapse."

The highway was liberally sprinkled with chain motels all around them. They chose the Wigwam Inn because of its silly neon sign of animated Indians dancing around a tepee. "Oh we must," she said. "It's just too wonderful." After they had checked into a whimsical double and had a good laugh at the furniture (especially the cow-hoof ashtray), Alexandra and Brandon pieced together Franklin's unpublished history as best they could.

Common to both accounts was the portrayal of the elder Sr. Corona as an industrious man of great passion who built a small home bakery into a profitable business. Implicit also was the feeling that Francisco, as spoiled children of formerly poor parents are wont to do, grew up thinking of his parents as ill bred, bourgeois, and embarrassing. Once he became successful, Sr. Corona became bored, alcoholic and abusive. In drunken rages he would beat his wife and child, once breaking little Francisco's arm in the process. The hurt and rage Francisco must have felt surfaced often at his Catholic school in schoolyard brawls and disruptive classroom behavior. According to Marlene, the nuns at his junior high expelled him three times before one Sister Maria Immaculata enticed him to join the boys' choir where Francisco found he had great talent as a tenor. "It was shortly after that, that Franklin developed the personality we came to know," observed Alexandra.

"Insensitive snob, you mean?" rejoined Brandon.

"Well, I suppose you could characterize him that way. It sounds to me like he channeled all his energies from his abusive home life to the comparative adulation he received in from music. Oh! And remember that girl Marlene said was strangled to death? At the time, the police thought Franklin did it."

"How did you find that out?"

"Well, we got to talking and one thing led to another and ... well, I told her that your father had once been arrested for murder."

Brandon laughed. "That's perfect! I told Matilda Chimoro he was an alcoholic!"

Alexandra scowled. "Why would you say something like that?"

"I wanted her to talk about old Mr. Corona's drinking. What's the matter? You told a lie about Dad, too, to get Frank's mother to talk."

"No, I didn't," she said. "Your father was arrested many, many times for murder. So many times in fact, the neighbors started suspecting I was having an affair with the bail bondsman."

Brandon had to nip this story in the bud. "So what happened to Franklin?"

"Nothing," she sighed. "They didn't have any evidence. But you have to agree we're seeing a clearer picture here."

"We are?"

"Yes. It's a classic story. We have a father who beat his wife – and child. That sort of abuse in inherited. It passes from generation to generation. I would think that it's highly likely that Franklin might have had the tendency to raise his hand to a female companion now and again."

"Well, that would be hard to prove, and besides, who cares? What would that have to do with Ethan being accused of Franklin's murder?"

Alexandra shrugged and walked to close the curtains in an effort to curtail the blinking pink glare of the neon sign. "Oh, I don't know," she said. "You found a woman murdered by someone obviously violent to women. We have another victim who may have been violent to women himself. Little pieces. Peggy Martinez, an old girlfriend, strangled. Maybe they go together; maybe they don't. Hand me a quarter, sweetheart."

Brandon did a double-take. "What for?"

"It says here, for twenty-five cents my bed will give me a soothing, vibrating massage. Frankly from the looks of these sheets, I'd be prepared to pay double if it didn't give me anything at all."

CHAPTER TEN

The moment their car pulled back into Taos, Brandon said, "I have to see Ethan."

Indeed, Brandon had a great need to see Ethan Arnold in jail. He hoped that if he told Ethan about how he was trying to prove his innocence, it might help relieve the guilt he felt for not coming out of the closet and giving him an alibi. He kept trying for the past two days not to imagine what it was like for Ethan behind bars but his mind freely leapt to the most bizarre and cruel pictures it could muster. Jail. It was such an upsetting concept for Brandon. He'd seen prisons in the movies and on television, but couldn't really believe those Hollywood slammers bore any relation to what the real world held in store for Ethan. Surely it must be an awful place, more awful than even his mind could, or would, at that moment imagine.

Worst of all was the image of the lone white toilet sitting out in the open in the middle of the cell. To Brandon, who was pee-shy in even the most private of places, the toilet in the open represented the cruelest indignity of all. Yes, he had to go to Ethan. He had to see for himself how Ethan was being treated, and replace his wild imagining with more comfortable, concrete facts, no matter how horrible the comfortable facts may be.

"Yes, perhaps that would be an excellent idea," said Alexandra. Brandon jumped with a start from the sound of her voice. It had taken her so long to answer him that he'd completely forgotten he had spoken to his mother in the first place.

"What? Oh. Yes, I think it's a good idea, too. I need to see if he's all right."

"Well of course," she added, "and you can take advantage of the visit to ask him a few questions."

"Like what? Like, hey Ethan, did you really kill Franklin?"

"Well, no. That would be a conversation stopper, don't you think? No, something more practical to ask him are smaller things. Things like why didn't he and Franklin get along the last time he stayed here. That might be useful to know."

"And P.J.!" exclaimed Brandon, with eyes wide with remembrance.

"Who?"

"P.J.," said Brandon again. "Remember at the pot luck? The night of the murder? I was eavesdropping on Ethan and P.J. Apparently P.J. was late because he tried – and failed – to do something."

"To do what?"

"I don't know what, but it apparently was something fairly important and secretive, and Ethan was disappointed in him and said he'd take care of it himself if he had to. When he left the party early, I assumed he was off to do whatever it was that P.J. failed to do first."

Alexandra gave him a slow stare of exasperation, eyes narrowed and mouth more rosebud by the second. "And you're just now remembering this, darling?"

"Well ... yes. I was curious about it at the party, but then so much happened right afterward that ..."

"You really should tell all this to the police," she said.

"No!" he snapped. "I'm not going to tell the police anything that might incriminate Ethan."

"Why not? What if it turns out that he really is to blame for this awful incident? Then how would you feel?"

"He's not! How can you say such a thing? Ethan had nothing to do with Franklin's death."

"Honestly, darling, I don't believe he killed poor Franklin either, but all I'm saying is you really can't be absolutely certain unless you were there, now can you?"

"Actually," Brandon said after a breath, "I am the only person who can be absolutely certain."

Alexandra laughed and said, "If you're trying to tell me that you killed Franklin Crown-Smith, I'd like you to tell me how you managed it since I was by your side all that night."

"That's not what I meant."

"Then what did you mean?"

Brandon opened his mouth to tell her he had spent the night of the murder with Ethan, then when no sounds came out, closed it and looked at Alexandra with such an odd expression that she became concerned and laid a comforting hand on his arm. "Is there something you want to tell me sweetheart?" she asked.

Brandon quickly gathered his composure and shook his head. "I really don't want to talk now," he said while turning toward the door. "I'm going over to the jail to see Ethan, I'll see you later. By the way, what do you want to do about dinner tonight?"

"Oh, leave it to me. I'll see if I can get us invited somewhere," she said with a smile. "Do you want the keys to the car?"

"No, I'll walk," he replied and stepped through the squeaky screen door which punctuated his exit with an inappropriately snappy exclamation point as it banged shut.

The county courthouse on South Pueblo Road in Taos was a fairly modern brick structure of cascading levels and few windows. It had the faux Pueblo look that was pretty much mandatory for all buildings of any size in Taos and Santa Fe. Despite its architectural nod toward the Pueblo, the courthouse, which held the town's incarceration facilities, was a shamelessly modern affair, reminiscent of public buildings in other western cities. What gave it that real Taos feel, though, was the vacant lot next to it, home to a large and loud prairie dog town.

Brandon's walk through Dog Town caused quite a stir among the little residents. Upon seeing him, the elders chirped out their warning cries to the younger dogs playing furiously in the open. With a chorus of squeals and yips and pattering prairie dog feet, the whole town vanished in less than two seconds flat. Brandon was actually a bit perturbed that the adorable little rodents found harmless-old-him to be any threat whatsoever. Noting quickly that it was silly to be offended by a prairie dog, he set his mind instead on what was to come as he approached the side entrance to the courthouse.

Once on the other side of the heavy aluminum door, he realized from the sudden level of silence in the court building just how noisy little Taos really was. Coolness, fluorescent light, and quiet were all that confronted him once inside. Well, coolness, quiet, and a guard behind a counter.

The guard, a policeman on desk duty, was fortyish, white, and round, with a face filled with bumpy, doughy features. His grey-brown shirt and trousers had obviously been issued when the officer was thinner, as now his girth inflated the fabric like an overfilled balloon.

"Can I visit someone you have in jail here?" Brandon asked. The uniformed man leaned back in his spring-backed chair, reaching behind him for a clipboard. The stretch pulled his shirt so tight over his protruding belly that Brandon winced to protect his eyes lest police buttons should pop like bullets in his face. The desk guard, with attire unexploded, grabbed the clipboard and slid it toward Brandon on the desk with a pen.

"You family?" he asked.

"Well, no," answered Brandon with surprise. "Does that matter?"

"Not partic'erly. Write your name and address and show me some photo I.D." Brandon complied by signing in as a resident of the Pembroke Colony and proffered a Pennsylvania driver's license. "Go through this door here," directed the desk guard, "and take the first left and then another left. Ask for Sergeant Cigarette and tell him who you want to see."

"Sergeant Cigarette?"

"You want me to write it down?"

"No," said Brandon, "I think I can handle that much," and he left to find the man with such a bizarre name.

After a pair of lefts, he was unexpectedly confronted with the large, brown, muscle-bound policeman that he noticed during the night of Ethan's arrest. "I'm looking for Sergeant Cigarette," Brandon said and the human wall acknowledged that it was he.

After only a surprisingly short delay, Brandon was led into a brightly lit, sparely apportioned room with cream painted cinder block walls with mint green accent stripes at wainscot height. Two tables with two chairs each were all the furniture and the only window (with that irritating chicken wire embedded in it) looked out into the hallway.

Brandon nervously entered and sat alone beneath the buzz of the fluorescent light until Ethan appeared at the door followed by another officer. Ethan was clad in a shapeless blue-gray jump suit, and looked, from the drawn expression on his face, much older than he was. The guard stood mute by the door as Ethan sat opposite Brandon and the two men stared at each other without speaking for a full minute. Finally, Brandon leaned forward and said sotto voce, "So is he going to keep standing there the whole time or what?"

Ethan slowly smiled and looked over at the stoic guard at the door. "Don't mind Kenny. Kenny and I are inseparable these days, aren't we Kenny?" Officer Kenny did not acknowledge that he was being spoken to. "Kenny's the silent type. You should see him when we're alone, though. He's an animal."

Brandon smiled and relaxed. "Are you okay? Are they treating you all right? Is it really awful?"

Ethan shrugged, "I'm okay. All things considered. I'm surprised to see you."

"Why?"

"I haven't really seen you since that night. I thought maybe …"

The flimsy retaining wall holding back Brandon's flood of guilt suddenly burst. "Listen, I'm so sorry. I'm sorry. I'm sorry I haven't been here before now. I'm sorry I didn't tell anybody that I was over at your place the night Franklin was killed, but it's hard for me …"

"I know."

"No, really. I'm such a wuss. I don't know what I'm afraid of; you've probably told the police everything anyway, right?"

"I said I wasn't alone that night. I didn't say your name, though."

"You didn't? How come?"

"It would probably end up in the papers and it's nobody's business. It's not important."

"Of course it's important. I'm your alibi. See, I had this plan that if I could find some other way to prove you were innocent, I wouldn't have to tell anybody about what we did. Mom and I actually started doing our own detective work, but it's so stupid. What was I thinking? Did I really think we could just go out and 'find' the real killer? And Mom's treating it like shopping! It would be easier if I just went in there right now and told whoever that during the murder you and I were having sex …"

Ethan reached across the table and took Brandon by the hand. "It doesn't matter."

"Yes, it does," said Brandon.

"No, it wouldn't make any difference. Really," Ethan said. "I found out this morning Frank was killed during the party."

Brandon thought about this for a moment then drew his hand away. "And you left the party early," he said quietly.

Ethan nodded. "So now what do you think?"

"I think … I don't know."

"Were you really out doing your own little investigation?"

Brandon nodded.

Ethan chuckled at the thought. "That's very sweet, Brandon. Thank you," he said then looked at Brandon with a sad, clear understanding. "But now you're thinking maybe I did do it. Maybe I did kill Frank. Maybe I stole those photos. I don't blame you. I get the newspapers in here. I read what they said about me."

"I don't care," said Brandon. "Just because you may have done stuff in the past, well … at least I don't think it means you're guilty now, does it?"

"What do you think? Do you think I stole the pictures at least?"

Brandon took a breath in to say of course not, but the words caught in his throat at the last second. Ethan eyed him coolly as Brandon finally stuttered, "Well … no, not necessarily …"

"I didn't do it," said Ethan flatly. "I have no idea how those Ansel Adams got behind the couch. I didn't put them there."

"I didn't think so," said Brandon with relief.

"No. I'm wrong," continued Ethan. "I know who set me up like this, but I'll be damned if I can prove it."

"Who?" asked Brandon.

"Franklin."

"What?"

"I found the pictures there behind my couch right after I got home from the pot luck. They were barely hidden. You could see them sticking out."

"I didn't see them."

"In your condition, you couldn't see much."

Brandon had to admit this was true. "Well, yeah. Okay," he said. "But why do you think it was Franklin who put them there?"

Ethan's eyes turned down to the lower left as he reflected and chose his words carefully. "My door was locked. My windows were latched from the inside. He had copies of all our keys. He was the only one who knew I stole some Ansel Adams prints years ago. And I was the only one who had dirt on him. PopIris knew I knew things about Franklin, and she must have told him."

Brandon suddenly felt his mother's chromosomes well up inside him like a tidal bore. "Oh, yeah?" he said leaning forward conspiratorially. "What did you know?"

Ethan sat back in his chair, almost as if he were pressed gingerly backward by Brandon's curiosity. He did not speak right away, but glanced at his stern friend Kenny, then slowly leaned forward to Brandon, elbows on the table. "I know why," Ethan said very slowly and very softly, "I know why Franklin Crown-Smith had to leave New York. And I know why he had to take this crummy job out in the middle of nowhere. I told Moira what I knew, and she must've gone running to Franklin. That's why he used the Adams prints to get me out of his hair. You saw how they tried using these little technicalities to evict me, and when that didn't work, he took down his photos, unlocked my door and put them behind my couch."

"But why?" said Brandon with his brows in a nervous knot. "What did you have on him?"

Ethan breathed in deeply through his nose and said matter-of-factly, "One day in New York, Franklin's girlfriend didn't show up for an understudy rehearsal because she was dead."

"So what are you saying?" asked Brandon. "Are you saying that he killed her?"

"No, I'm not saying anything," said Ethan. "I'm just telling you what I know. It was no secret to anybody he'd given her a black eye the week before. Then she dies and he suddenly skips town."

"So did the police suspect him? Why wasn't he arrested?"

Ethan shrugged. "I don't know. I think he had an alibi, but he was questioned, all right."

"So how come nobody else knows anything about this? Shouldn't it have been in the newspapers at the time?"

"It didn't get much coverage. Officially it was a burglary gone wrong, or something. No one in New York was really interested."

Brandon mulled this gossip for a second then became increasingly perplexed. "So how did you know all this stuff?"

"I used to live in Chelsea with a lover who was on the arts staff of the New York Times. He dug up all sorts of dirt on Franklin, but the Times wouldn't print it because my friend didn't have enough proof and they were afraid of a lawsuit. My boyfriend told me everything. I had so much dirt on Franklin Crown-Smith he could've dammed the Rio Grande with it."

"Jesus," said Brandon, "did Franklin know this before he accepted you at the Pembroke?"

"No. I don't think so. He must have thought everything was forgotten when he nipped off to New Mexico."

"Have you told all this to your lawyer?"

"What lawyer? I still don't have one," he said. "They're having trouble finding some idiot to appoint."

"Well, make sure you tell him this stuff when you get one."

"Time to go," said Kenny the Guard from his post by the door.

"All right," said Brandon as he stood up to leave, "I'll be going. But just tell me two things, Ethan," he added quickly.

"What?"

"What was his girlfriend's name and how was she killed?"

Ethan remained seated and closed his eyes in thought. He ran a hand across his high forehead then nodded and opened his eyes. "Susan Lalo," he said assuredly. "And she was strangled."

As he started home, Brandon did an about-face in the middle of Prairie Dog Town. The murder of Susan Lalo. It was another link in the chain of events leading up to Ethan's arrest. It seemed to Brandon that he ought to try to learn a little more about Susan Lalo before presenting all he had just learned to his mother. She would have thousands of questions to catapult at him and he would feel better knowing a better response than a shrug.

Although the Taos Public Library would probably be a bust as far as any non-local information was concerned, it was really the only option he could think of that was within walking distance. Being late in the afternoon, Brandon hoped at the very least it would just be open. Anything more than that would be icing.

As it turned out, Brandon arrived a good fifteen minutes before the end of the library day. He wasted no time wandering around the building, but went right for the small checkout desk right inside the front hallway.

A solidly built young man of clearly Spanish lineage stood behind the desk reading a citation into a telephone. He was very young, high school age probably, and had a post adolescent overachiever air of confidence in the information he was imparting. Brandon remembered the type well from his own days at school. Being at the artistic-nerd end of the school pariah spectrum, he had often envied the intellectual-nerds for their ability to navigate the most complex world/universal issues while being totally defeated by the simple politics of high school life. Just watching this library boy talk on the phone made Brandon feel easy and confident that he had indeed come just to the right place.

It was not long until the young man hung up the phone. Before Brandon had a chance to get his attention, he turned abruptly with a stack of four plainly bound reference books and left to replace them in their proper place on the shelves. Anal retentive, thought Brandon, using one of the only half-dozen remaining concepts he remembered from freshman psychology. He's methodical and orderly … like Mother.

The library was practically empty and the sounds in the silent room became more pronounced. The soft buzz of the old fluorescent tubes, the steady undertone hum of the pole fan in the corner, and the muted pat of hard sole shoes on aging linoleum all heralded the end of the day at the library. Brandon's young fellow returned, this time carrying a light jacket in his hand and a paper bag with what appeared to be the remains of a sack lunch.

"Can I help you" he asked Brandon. "We're just about to close."

"Well, I uh, I don't know," said Brandon suddenly tongue-tied. How would he explain to a stranger what he was looking for? What if this boy asked him why? "Do you have back issues of The New York Times or any other New York papers?"

"Are you kidding?" said the boy with a laugh. "We've got The Albuquerque Journal and The Santa Fe New Mexican on microfilm and about a year's worth of The Taos News in paper. And we're lucky to have that. Why? What do you need?"

Brandon let defeat grab him quickly and decided to make a hasty retreat. "Oh, nothing. I was just trying to get a copy of an old news story."

Just as Brandon started to go, the boy called after him, "Do you know the date?"

Brandon turned back and saw that the boy was putting on his coat, clearly not intending to stay. "No," he said, "it was probably about ten years ago."

"In New York?"

"Yes."

"You mean like a story about 9/11?"

Brandon hadn't thought of that. It was probably significant that no one so far had told any terrorism-related stories. "No," he said. "I think it must have happened a year or so before that."

"Well, do you have a name or some other kind of search criteria?"

"Um … well, yes."

The boy thought it over briefly and rolled down the top of his paper lunch sack to make a better handle. The paper crackled loudly in the empty room. "You can get all that on the Internet."

"Can I use the computers here? I don't have any way to get on the Web where I'm staying."

"No, we're closing. But you can come over to my house and we can do whatever you want."

"Excuse me?" said Brandon, a bit startled, not knowing what sort of proposition the young man had in mind.

"You can search on my computer," said the boy. "The New York Times has an online archive going back a hundred years."

"That's great!" said Brandon, relieved. "Could we do it right now?"

"Sure. Are you parked nearby?"

"I don't have a car."

"Oh," he said with a bit of disappointment, "me neither. It's about a twenty minute walk if you don't mind."

"After you," said Brandon and followed his young friend out.

On the way to the boy's home, Brandon found out his name was Thomas Muñoz, or just Thommy (with an H) and that indeed he was a senior at Taos High. Thommy lived on the extreme north of Taos with his mother who was a chamber maid at the Kachina Lodge. After graduation, he had plans to go to UNM in Albuquerque to take a double major in English Lit and Computer Science. Apparently, he had some sort of inexplicable further plan to combine the two in an academic career.

Thommy's house was of the old standard adobe variety, similar to the artists' cottages surrounding the Pembroke. Like most of the homes in town, it had no grass in the front or back yard, but was fronted with a reasonably well managed assortment of rocks, wild plants, dirt, and a besieged flower bed. Once inside the dark, cool house, Brandon noted the slip covered furniture, the ancient scatter rugs and the profusion of Muñoz family religious and personal artifacts huddling for safety on every inch of available tabletop and wall.

Mamma Muñoz was not at home, so unimpeded, they slipped directly into Thommy's small back bedroom which originally was a patio that had been enclosed with cheap paneling, good intentions, and very little skill.

"It must get pretty cold in here in the wintertime," observed Brandon as he stood uncomfortably in the center of the room, not knowing quite what to do with himself. Thommy's room, unlike the part of the house they had just passed through, was a model of almost military efficiency in its austere emptiness. The bed was made so tightly that the sheets and blankets looked spray-printed on. Other than a lone hardback chair at a cheap metal desk, there was nowhere else to sit.

"Go ahead and sit on the bed," Thommy offered. "I don't mind."

Brandon nodded and smiled as he gingerly rested his rear on the edge of the mattress, trying hard not to mess up the bedspread (as if he could). Thommy hung his coat carefully in a homemade armoire in the corner then removed a brown fabric dust cover from the personal computer on his desk. It was a conglomeration of mismatched and outdated pieces of used PC parts. Thommy sat down and switched the computer on and much to Brandon's surprise, it beeped and revved up almost instantly. He had never seen a clone computer boot so fast.

"Okay, let's go to the Times Web site," said Thommy. "Give me some key words to search with."

"Why don't you just try 'Susan Lalo' and see what happens?"

Thommy typed the name into the search box. "Well, that was easy," he said. "You said it was more than ten years ago? How about 1998?"

"Yeah, could be. Why?"

"Jackpot," he said. "There's one here that says: 'Singer Slain in Apparent Robbery Attempt.' And another one that goes: 'No clues in Opera Strangle.' Creepy, huh? You want me to email them to you?"

"Can you just print them out?"

Thommy looked uncertainly at his small, cheap printer, shrugged and said, "Sure, I guess."

"I'll give you twenty bucks for a new printer cartridge, don't worry," said Brandon with a smile. Thommy beamed and printed off the articles.

Brandon slipped Tommy a twenty and shook his hand before quickly skimming the copy. "Thank you so much," he said, flipping pages. "This is perfect! 'Susan Lalo, a member of the Opera West! Company currently appearing at Lincoln Center's

State Theater was found strangled late yesterday in her 314 West 45th Street ... apartment ... Oh my god."

"What's the matter?" asked Thommy.

"That's Moira's address," said Brandon.

CHAPTER ELEVEN

It was getting close to 6:30 by the time Brandon came bounding through the screen door of his adobe house. His mother was seated on the sofa dressed in a camel brown cowl neck sweater and white slacks, looking for all the world like she was about to receive important company any minute.

All the way home from Thommy's, he had been rehearsing in his head just how he'd relate to Alexandra everything that he'd learned that afternoon. It was important how information was fed to his mother: one vague fact and she'd be all over him; one illogical sequence of events and she'd interrupt him so many times he'd forget half of everything and end up babbling incoherently like a drunkard. Upon seeing her quietly seated on the sofa, he dove immediately into the prepared opening of his speech without even saying hello.

"You and I have to sit down and seriously rethink our impressions of the murder night," he declared.

Alexandra's eyes widened and she looked a bit uncomfortable. "Um, sweetheart ..." she began.

Brandon held up a traffic cop hand and stopped her from speaking. "No, let me finish. I found out a lot of stuff this afternoon. A lot of stuff." He emphasized this last phrase by casually waving the printouts in front of Alexandra's perplexed expression. "Ethan's innocent. Completely innocent. He's in jail because of a frame-up job that Franklin pulled right before he was killed."

Alexandra cleared her throat. Brandon continued head-on, gaining momentum as he went along. "Ethan is convinced that Franklin hid the photos behind the sofa so he could get rid of Ethan who knows too much about Franklin's past. Ethan's got all sorts of dirt on Franklin. Lots of mean little nasty stuff sure, but also big stuff, too. Like maybe even a possible murder that Franklin could have committed."

At this news, Alexandra once again cleared her throat quite forcefully and said, "Aren't you even going to say hello?"

Brandon was stopped in his tracks by this strange remark. "Oh, well, yes. Hello, Mother," he said.

"I meant to Iris," she said and nodded behind and just to the left of Brandon. He turned around and noticed for the first time that PopIris Nelson was sitting behind the open front door on the lumpy old chair by the rat-trunk.

Sitting stiff-spined in a plain navy dress, PopIris had no expression discernible to Brandon at all. The black glass eye beneath the bangs of her limp haircut reflected the foursquare pattern of the front window in blind comment to Brandon's rudeness.

"Oh, hello Iris," he said, quickly reviewing what he had just said to his mother hoping to high hell that he hadn't spilled any beans of import on Miss Nelson.

"So you've been to see Ethan Arnold," said PopIris in a coolly conversational way.

"Uh, yes," he said, surprised at her manner. "Over at the courthouse."

"And how is he?"

"He's fine. Well, under the circumstances, you know. But now come to think of it, he's surprisingly fine considering the circumstances, which is odd."

Alexandra rose and stood next to her son. "Not really," she said. "Ethan seemed like a rather stable, resilient fellow."

"Yes," agreed PopIris. "And you're right when you say that Franklin never liked him. I always wondered why, but now … it would make a lot of sense if what you said is true."

"Oh, it's true, all right," insisted Brandon as he hid the computer printouts casually behind his back, hoping that PopIris would forget that he had waved them about earlier, but of course that was hardly likely. There was an almost zen-like serenity about Iris that evening. So unlike herself. Sitting there, she exuded a friendly stillness that on anyone else would have been considered poise, but on PopIris seemed to smack of deception of some indefinable sort. Anyway, Brandon and Alexandra both knew instinctively that PopIris was looking to pump them for news about Franklin as eagerly as they were looking to pump her.

Alexandra, who had the strongest conversational pump handle, said to Brandon, "I ran into Iris just an hour ago down on the Plaza and we both thought it would be a delightful idea if we had dinner together this evening."

"Great," said Brandon, trying a bit too hard to look genuinely pleased."

"At first I offered to cook something here, but Iris mentioned she knew of a place nearby that she says we have to try before we leave Taos."

"The Black Moon," said PopIris. "It's very small, known mostly to locals. A couple run it out of their carport on the side of their house. Just four or five tables. Very charming and Mrs. Fernandez is a marvel. Franklin and I go there – used to go there, often."

"Sounds great," agreed Brandon, taking a step backward toward his bedroom. "I'll go wash up." He turned smoothly and transferred the computer pages to his chest away from Iris as he left the room. Once out of their sight, Brandon carefully folded the papers in half and slid them under his clean underwear in the top drawer of his bedroom dresser. He dressed quickly, being sure to wear something more or less the same tone of Alexandra's outfit. Brandon had learned at a very young age the folly of wearing whatever he wanted when his mother was around. No pair of jeans was worth the abuse.

PopIris was correct in describing the Black Moon as a converted carport. Attached to the side of a brown Taos house, the little restaurant was crude and dark, but somehow magical. The floor was concrete, painted glossy black with white paint spattered throughout that gave diners the feeling of walking on stars. The walls were plywood painted a deep violet and azure and had moons, many, many ceramic moons, glazed glossy black, hanging everywhere. By the light of fifteen candles on the five little tables, the room looked as through gypsies might be ready to burst through the door any moment to saw out a mazurka on dueling violins, but the music was Spanish and low and coming from a radio.

A somber woman with a bouffant head of gray curls greeted them at the door and led them to a table at the back corner of the little dining room. The tablecloth was of blue and black check and the ashtray was a moon of black.

"This is charming," cooed Alexandra.

"Thank you, Juana," said PopIris to their hostess. Juana did not smile, but looked bored and efficient as she helped push in both Alexandra and Brandon's chairs (which Brandon found embarrassing since PopIris didn't get a push).

Once her guests were seated, Juana said, "You want it now or do you want to wait?"

Brandon and Alexandra looked perplexed and turned to PopIris for guidance. "Now, Juana, would be fine," she said and Juana left.

"Want what now?" asked Alexandra nonchalantly to PopIris who seemed to know the lingo.

"Dinner," said PopIris. "It takes forever to eat here so I thought we'd start it now."

"Aren't we going to get menus?" asked Brandon peering at the other diners.

"Aren't any," said PopIris. "They tell you what to eat here."

"I beg your pardon?" said Alexandra.

PopIris kindly explained, "It's table d'hôte. Her husband makes whatever he feels like each day. All you have to do is show up here and be served."

"But how do we know we'll like it?" asked Brandon, ill at ease with such a concept.

"Oh, you'll like it," assured PopIris. "As long as you never ask what anything is or how much it costs. Usually they don't even know themselves. Many of the foods don't translate well into English and as for the prices … well, they just make it up as they go. The bill is always a surprise."

"Oh, fine," groaned Brandon, who was now twenty dollars poorer thanks to the assistance of Thommy Muñoz.

"And anyway, this is all on me," said PopIris.

"No!" said Alexandra. "Don't be silly. You don't have to do this."

"But I want to," PopIris insisted. "You've been so very kind through this terrible time. I wanted to find a way to say thank you."

"But you can't afford this," insisted Alexandra. "And besides, I've been hesitating to ask but … are you still employed now that …"

"Now that Franklin is gone? Probably not. The board will hire a new director and the new director will probably hire a new assistant. Anyway, it's doubtful I'd stay even if asked. I'm eager to return to New York."

PopIris was holding herself together until she was goaded into saying Franklin's name aloud. The slight hesitation and quaver in her voice belied her outward sangfroid and alluded to the depth of her feeling toward her employer. "You'd been with Franklin quite a long time, haven't you?" said Alexandra.

"Over fifteen years."

"Do you think you'll stay in the same field or do you think you'll move on to something new?"

PopIris breathed in slowly and tucked a loose strand of hair behind her ear. "Well, it's a little late to resume my first career. Back in 1983, right after I got out of high school, I moved to New York and danced with a small company until I had my accident. I was married briefly, then took a job in artist management."

"A dancer! I should have known by the way you carried yourself. I bet you were marvelous! Ballet?"

"Yes," admitted PopIris, looking uncomfortably self-conscious. "I was only in the corps; I never soloed."

Brandon said, "The loss of your eyesight must have made doing the turns and stuff too difficult, right?"

PopIris looked at him blankly with her good eye and said, "I broke my leg in a car collision. I was born with one eye."

Brandon blanched and determined not to open his mouth again until he was very, very old. Alexandra wished the same for her son.

"So you worked for an agent?" she asked, trying to quickly divert PopIris to a new topic.

"Yes. For the fine arts. That was how I got the job with Franklin. We started to represent Opera West! in the mid 'seventies. I didn't like working at the agency and Franklin made me an offer."

"How marvelous. Were you in Paris?"

"Oh, yes. I was there for the Paris Opera in '96. I negotiated the deal. I negotiated all their contracts and was in charge of all their bookings. Opera West! was my complete focus."

"Franklin must have relied on you heavily."

"We were a team," she said simply. "He couldn't have done anything without me. He handled the artistic end of things exclusively, but the success of Opera West! as a profitable and respected company was mine."

Juana returned to the table carrying a tray with glasses of water and steaming bowls of green lumps swimming in black liquid. Brandon stared silently into his dish as it was placed before him and tried to discern whether the green lumps were formally of the plant or (god forbid) animal kingdom. Alexandra had on her "gracious face" while Juana Fernandez was in view, enigmatic to all but Brandon. He could tell his mother was biding her time to comment until "the help" was out of earshot. As Juana disappeared out the door again, Brandon and Alexandra looked imploringly toward each other, then back at their bowls, then burst into laughter. PopIris was nonplussed.

"Did I miss something amusing?" she dead-panned.

"What is this?" asked Brandon, trying to control his laughter.

Alexandra composed herself and rejoined, "Yes, dear. What exactly have we here?"

PopIris looked down at her first course thoughtfully for a moment. "I have no idea" she admitted. Brandon and Alexandra erupted into laughter once more and PopIris even was forced to crack a smile at the food. Bravely they each lifted a spoonful of the unidentifiable to their lips and were rewarded with the flavor of perhaps the finest soup in the state of New Mexico.

"Earlier, you mentioned to your mother that the two of you would have to rethink the events of the night Franklin died," said PopIris. Brandon and Alexandra said nothing, but smiled noncommittally and tried to appear oh-so-interested in their green lump soup. "I'd be curious to hear what exactly went on that night," she continued. "No one's told me a thing about that party and I'd be interested to hear what you thought really happened."

"Alexandra put down her spoon and dabbed her lips, then gave PopIris a sad, long look of friendly concern. "So what would you like to know?"

"Who could have done this thing?" asked PopIris.

"Anyone," replied Alexandra. "All of us had an opportunity to sneak away ... well, almost all of us. Brandon and I were together all evening. The boy, P.J., came late. Ethan left early."

"Lorna and Brian went out to the store together."

Alexandra nodded. "Yes, and GooGoo L'Amour ..."

"Moira."

"... yes, Moira was, well, she was there the whole time we were there, and we were there the whole time. She was never out of our sight.

"Or was she?" asked Brandon.

"What do you mean?" asked PopIris.

"Was she really there the whole time, or did we just think she was there the whole time?"

Alexandra went back to her soup and asked casually, "Why the sudden interest in Moira?"

"Well ... oh, I don't know."

Alexandra looked over at PopIris who looked at Brandon like a cat outside the window of a fish market. "You can speak freely in front of Iris, dear."

"Oh, yes. Do," said PopIris.

"Perhaps she can help answer any questions about Moira you have."

"I'd be glad to help if I can."

"Actually, maybe you can," admitted Brandon. "When I spoke to Ethan this afternoon in jail, he told me about something that happened to Franklin thirteen years ago. In New York in 1998, I heard that Franklin's fiancée was murdered in her apartment. Do you remember anything about that at all, Iris?"

"Oh yes, of course," she said with perfect equanimity. "They said she walked in on a burglar."

"Yes, well. I went by the Taos Public Library after I saw Ethan and I met this boy with a computer who got me reprints of the newspaper stories. They did say that it was an apparent burglary."

"Why did Ethan tell you about this?" asked Alexandra.

"Because," continued Brandon, "What the newspapers didn't print was the fact that Franklin was notorious for beating the poor girl to a pulp on a regular basis."

"Oh, dear," his mother clucked.

"Those were only rumors," said an indignant PopIris. "That girl, whatever her name was …"

"Susan Lalo."

"Yes, Susan Lalo, was notorious for being a liar at Opera West! and no, she was not Franklin's fiancée. That was another bizarre story she concocted just to get special attention in the company."

"Well that's interesting," said Brandon. "But the most interesting thing of all was Susan Lalo's address."

"And what about it?" pressed Alexandra.

"It's Moira's New York address."

"Is that all?" laughed his mother. "Same apartment and everything?"

Brandon was deflated. "I … I don't know. The street address is the same. They didn't mention the apartment."

"And how long has Moira lived at that address?"

"I don't know," repeated Brandon with a sheepish can-you-help-me? look to PopIris.

"Don't look at me," said PopIris. "I never heard of the woman before she applied to the Pembroke earlier this year."

"And besides, even if she were connected to that woman all those years ago, that still doesn't alter the fact that Moira did not leave the party the night of the murder."

"Well, I didn't think she did either," countered Brandon, "but I was interested in trying to see if there was perhaps something that evening that happened, something small – like that thing I overheard P.J. saying – that we forgot about. Are we sure Moira was there all night?"

"Positive," said Alexandra. "I remember the evening perfectly. Moira was in the kitchen when we got there and then was either in the living room with us the rest of the evening or locked in the bathroom washing off all that blood."

"I beg your pardon?" said PopIris.

"Oh never mind," assured Alexandra. "Performance art. It defies description."

"She was in there a hell of a long time, too," noted Brandon.

"Yes, but we could hear her the whole time in there singing and splashing around.

Brandon nodded in reluctant agreement and splashed his spoon around in his soup for a moment. "So there's still the mystery of P.J." he said. "He had plenty of time and opportunity to kill Franklin, although as far as we know, he had precious little reason to do so."

"He and Ethan are fairly chummy," noted Alexandra.

"So?" said Brandon in an accusatory tone.

"So if Ethan had motives, then P.J. – being close to Ethan – might have motives, too."

"But Ethan does not," he countered.

Alexandra paused and reflected. "Well then, look at it this way: not only did P.J. have time to commit the murder, he also had time to see the murder committed. Possibly. Or see something that would be helpful in solving this mess."

PopIris had been sitting silently, taking all this in. "That boy was a very interesting case," she said. "Franklin heard about him from the Poet Laureate at Kentucky State University. The boy is supposed to be some sort of idiot savant in the world of poetry. Practically no education whatsoever, functionally illiterate, comes up with volumes of verse out of nowhere. Nobody can figure him out. Franklin offered this residency to him sight unseen. He didn't even apply to us."

"Not a great reason to kill, is it?" said Brandon. "Ethan had been working with him in the afternoons all summer. P.J. would dictate to him and Ethan would take it all down. That was mostly why they spent so much time together.

"Mostly?" asked Alexandra. "I assumed, and tell me if I'm wrong, that there was a bit of a romantic interest there between those two. As I said, tell me if I'm wrong."

PopIris looked uncomfortable with the suggestion and said simply, "Well, I wouldn't know."

Brandon, on the other hand, felt a little buzz go through him and didn't know quite what to say. "Well, um, I think there might have been, or is, some interest there, but I don't think they're anything more than friends. Ethan is so much older than P.J. I mean, something might have happened between them, but it might have been a one-time thing and ..."

"It was only a suggestion of an initial impression I had," said Alexandra. "As I said, I could be wrong. I loved his poem though. How did it go?"

No one said anything for a minute or two as Juana Fernandez cleared away the soup and filled the water tumblers. "She rises through the roof like smoke," said Brandon.

"I beg your pardon?" said PopIris.

"Yes. That was it," agreed Alexandra. "She rises through the roof like … she rises through the roof … oh my."

Brandon clarified for Iris, "It's the start of one of P.J.'s poems."

"She rises through the roof. Don't you get it, Brandon? He saw her."

"He saw who?"

"If his poems are mostly extemporaneous, it's likely he saw something unusual happening the night of the murder and made a poem about it right there in front of our eyes."

"Saw what?" said Brandon, mightily confused.

Alexandra turned to PopIris. "In Lorna's house, are you familiar with the bathroom?"

"Of course," she said. "Why?"

"There are no windows in her bathroom, are there?"

"No. No windows other than the skylight."

"Of course," she said, looking perfectly pleased. "She rises through the roof like smoke, while we think she's taking a long bath, she could be out anywhere."

Brandon cut her off before she could go any further, "But you yourself said we could hear her singing and splashing about."

Alexandra thought about this seriously and then her face brightened with realization. "She did take her tape player with her into the bathroom, didn't she?"

"I don't know," he said. "I couldn't say."

"Well, I could say," said Alexandra definitively. "She gathered up all her discarded costuming and props into a big bundle and skittered into the bathroom. She could have had a half hour worth of singing and splashing on the other side of the tape she used for accompaniment in her act. In fact, I'll bet you anything that was a one hour cassette, thirty minutes on each side."

Brandon started to get excited about the idea, then the black clouds of realization moved in. "So what we're sitting here thinking is that Moira, my friend, is some kind of malice-of-forethought cold blooded murderess?"

"Murderer, dear. Try not to be so sexist."

"No, I'm sorry. I don't buy it. I might have been about to believe it when I was thinking of this as something someone did in an act of passion. But to suggest that it was a well thought-out plan, an execution, that's where I draw the line. We were with Moira the next morning when we found Franklin. She seemed excited and shocked and asked lots of questions about everything. She didn't seem at all like someone who might have just killed somebody. She's just as interested as we are in finding out who did this."

"And she's an actress," stated Alexandra simply. "Or, rather, actor."

"No," said Brandon, "Let's drop this. I know Moira, and I just can't imagine her hanging somebody."

"Well, we do have a few things to find out before we can say either way. We have to find out what that murdered woman's apartment number was, and what Moira's apartment number was, and how long she was living there before we can point any fingers."

"I can help you there," said PopIris. "Although I couldn't begin to tell you anything about Susan Lalo, I'm sure we have all the other information you need on Miss Atchison."

But we've already got the photocopies, thought Brandon, but his mother said, "Would you be a dear, Iris, and look in your files for us tomorrow? I would be nice to erase all wild suspicions. I'm sure the address in that article is all just some strange coincidence."

"Of course it is," said PopIris. "If you want, you can stop by the office tomorrow morning."

Alexandra straightened up sharply and said, "Oh! I almost forgot! Brandon, while you were visiting Ethan, Lorna was by and invited us to a picnic in the gorge. Of course I accepted although I haven't a clue what in the world 'the gorge' is or how we plan to eat in it."

"Oh, you'll love it," said PopIris. "The Rio Grande cuts a beautiful, deep canyon just outside of the town. There are several nice spots for fishing and picnicking at the bottom. It's tricky to get down there, but the gorge is one of our most famous sites. I highly recommend it."

"When?" asked Brandon.

"Tomorrow morning," answered Alexandra. "Lorna, her fellow ..."

"Brian."

"... yes, Brian, and the boy ..."

"P.J."

"Of course, yes that's it, and Moira are all meeting at ten o'clock at the end of the drive. We're to ride in the back of Moira's truck on the hay."

Brandon winced. "Sounds ... interesting. Do you want to go?"

"Of course I want to go!" said Alexandra. "I have the perfect outfit to wear!"

"All right. How 'bout you, Iris? Are you up for a picnic in the gorge?"

PopIris Nelson looked none too comfortable at the suggestion and deferred politely with the statement, "I'm allergic to hay."

Nothing more was said that evening about the murder or about any other possible scenarios for murder. The meal continued with a course of salad, a course of pork, a course of flan, and of course, a course of conversation in the form of an endless Alexandra Bennington Peters Noble monologue that started with what seemed to Brandon like the creation of the universe and ended with his mother's exploits somewhere in the heart of Morocco, doing a dangerous bit of shopping in a bazaar adventure.

As promised, PopIris Nelson refused to hear any arguments when the check came and also refused to let Alexandra even see the amount that the check came to. In reality, Alexandra was perfectly at ease with the concept of having PopIris spring for the tab. Mostly she wanted to take a peek at the bill in hopes that there might be some indication on the slip of the name of whatever it was they had just eaten.

But no such luck.

CHAPTER TWELVE

It didn't surprise Brandon that Moira drove like a maniac. She was a New Yorker, after all. From what he could surmise, people from New York City only very rarely got a chance to sit behind the wheel of an automobile, and when they did, they considered things like traffic laws and pavement lines to be only abstract, insignificant concepts, easy enough to ignore. Careening down the canyon roads south of Taos, Moira took every curve with such heedless abandon that she gave all her passengers' digestive tracts that nice roller coaster sensation of terror mingled with a touch of mal-de-mer.

Counting Alexandra, only five members of the Pembroke Colony opted to go on the picnic at the Rio Grande Gorge State Park. Moira went because she was eager to take her rattletrap truck out for a proper spin. Lorna and Brian apparently needed the outing to give them a temporary rest from their latest round of constant bickering. Brandon didn't know why he and Alexandra were going. Among the absentees, P.J. Copeland did not come because he was suddenly nowhere to be found, and Glenda Guilder, covertly disliked by everyone, didn't show because she was not invited.

Irritatingly to Brandon, Alexandra had insisted on sitting in the back of the truck with Brian and him. Try as they might, no one could persuade Alexandra that she might be more comfortable with Moira in the cab, so Lorna climbed up front while Alexandra rode out in the open with the boys. Before they took off, she carved out a comfortable, scratchy niche in the hay right behind the driver. For safety's sake, she wrapped a rope around her waist and tied it to the walls of the truck to keep herself from getting blown out onto the road. For beauty's sake, she tied several scarves around her head to keep her hair from getting blown out of the truck, too.

With Moira's wild driving making him ill, Brandon was grateful that the trip wasn't very long. The Rio Grande Gorge State Park was only sixteen miles south of Taos. Once they got to the park turnoff, a series of heart-stopping switchbacks on a washed-out gravel road made even GooGoo L'Amour downshift and occasionally use her brake pedal. The road to the park plunged them down several hundred feet to the canyon floor below where there were a series of campgrounds with shelters, tables, fire pits and a spectacular view of the steep-sided gorge.

Shaken, bruised and deafened by the trip, Alexandra had to be helped from the truck when they arrived at the bottom of the canyon. Brandon's ears were ringing, too, when the truck finally stopped, but he quickly realized that the roar in his head was not from the torturous trip to the river, but rather from the roar of the Rio Grande itself.

The river was magnificent. Noisy as a stadium crowd, it thundered through the halls of the canyon, violently smashing itself around curves, into boulders, on its desperate rush to the Gulf of Mexico.

"We might see some white water rafters go by," exclaimed Moira as she unloaded the bags of food from the opened tailgate. "Maybe we should take a day and do a raft trip. The rafting company's just down the road in Pilar. Whadda you say, Lexy?"

"Lexy" shrugged with disinterest at the suggestion as she unwrapped her head. "Oh, I don't know," she said. "Once you've rafted down the Yang Tse, everything else pales."

Brian Epstein, looking incognito in his Mets cap and sunglasses, consulted a hiking map he had brought along and made an alternate suggestion. "There's a hiking trail from here that leads to the Box."

"The Box?" asked Brandon. "What's in the Box?"

"Let's Make a Deal! I loved that show!" chimed Moira, who wasn't listening very well.

"It's the place in the gorge where the canyon is the steepest and the highest," explained Brian, folding up his map. "I don't know why they call it the Box."

"Well, let's eat first," said Lorna a little sharply as she spread a cloth on a large and rotting picnic table anchored in concrete. "You always plan these hikes without ever knowing how long they'll take or even where you're going, and I always end up starving on some backwoods trail somewhere as it's starting to get dark."

"You don't have to go, if you don't want to," growled Brian.

"I didn't say I didn't want to go. I just said if you don't know where the hell you're going, I think it would be wiser to eat first. That's all I'm saying."

"It's a four or five mile hike here on the map! What is that? Maybe an hour each way, something like that. Jesus Lorna ..."

Brandon and Alexandra wanted to avoid their mounting squabble, so they took the opportunity to walk over to the edge of the river to pay their respects to the Rio Grande. It was a little difficult for Alexandra to climb over the rocks in her red espadrilles, but teetering furiously, she finally made it to the edge of the water. Brandon, supporting his mother so she wouldn't fall in, said, "Don't you think it's beautiful?"

"I probably look like the Bride of Frankenstein," she said, mashing down her hair.

"I was talking about the river."

"Remarking on the river is pointless," she said, "when my hair so desperately needs discussion."

Resisting the temptation to push her headfirst into the rapids, Brandon instead extended his arm to Alexandra and led her back to the picnic table by the truck.

Brian and Lorna had finished arguing and had started sulking by the time they returned. Lorna busied herself with lunch preparations as Moira sat across the table from Brian, idly listening to him propound on the arts.

"It's just meaningless form and movement," he was saying. "They described it as kinetic sculpture, which in my book is an oxymoron, but what it really was was just a couple of near-naked cheerleaders jumping around in slow motion. They even had the balls to call the piece Henry Moore – Or Less. What a bunch of idiots!"

Moira simply stared at him and said, "You've got the blackest hair I've ever seen."

Alexandra, seizing on something she could understand, stepped behind Brian and removed his baseball cap. "It's so thick and curly," she said running her fingers over his scalp. "Wouldn't you die to have hair like this, GooGoo?"

"In a minute," she agreed.

Brandon took Brian's hat away from his mother and returned it to its owner. "What were you talking about?" he asked Brian.

"Dance," said Lorna curtly. "We saw a dance group at a Next Wave festival in L.A."

"It was a piece of shit," said Brian.

Lorna, however, would not let him get away with an opinion quite that easily. "Brian, you're not a dancer. You don't know anything about dance. Why do you condemn everything you don't understand as shit?"

"You don't have to understand shit to smell it," he replied.

"If you don't understand something how can you have an opinion on it? You're constantly saying you don't want to see a certain movie, or read a certain book, or go to a certain play because it's shit. How do you know it's shit? How can you possibly say anything is shit if you don't see it? Or if you do see it, how can you judge anything that you could never in a million years do yourself? Who are you to judge somebody else's work as drivel?"

"I never said drivel. I said shit."

"You know, Brian, you drive me crazy sometimes! You're just like Frank!"

"You mean dead?" snorted Brian, replacing his cap on his head.

"Don't push me," hissed Lorna as she threw down the paper plates she was holding and stalked away from the group.

Alexandra sat next to Moira and whispered, "What was all that about?"

"I'll tell you later," she whispered back, and picked up the stack of paper plates. "Lu-unch!" said Moira in her cheeriest, sing-songy bell tones.

Lunch after that was a quiet affair. Lorna had gone off by herself on a long walk, leaving the others to awkwardly try to pursue some other topics of conversation.

"You have any performances planned when you get back to New York?" Brandon asked Moira.

"No," she said.

"Are you having any exhibitions of your sculptures soon?" Alexandra asked Brian.

"No," he said.

Anything was better than this, thought Brandon, so he was forced to use "the last resort." "So Mom," he said to her innocently, "do you have any trips planned?" And that was it.

"Oh, sweetheart, didn't I tell you? I'm going to Madagascar with Janet and Paul for the month of August."

"Why?" he asked.

"For the Antananarivo International Film Festival, of course," she said with surprise. "Surely you've heard of it. It's the largest black African French-speaking film festival in the southern hemisphere. Really, Brandon. Sometimes you surprise me." So at least they were saved from the fate of eating in silence as Alexandra did her damnedest to exhaust the topic of Madagascar, which turned out to be not quite as exhaustible as one would suppose.

Lorna Shaw was still off walking alone as they finished their picnic meal. Brandon, Alexandra, Brian and Moira waited a good half hour before deciding to leave her to fend for herself. They packed up almost all of the food, sealing it against any scavenging animals that might wander by and then, two-by-two, they started out on the rocky hiking trail that led from the picnic area to the Box of the Rio Grande Gorge.

Alexandra, walking behind the two men with Moira at her side, had the good forethought to change into proper footwear, but even with pricey hiking shoes on her feet, she deliberately made slow progress as they walked along. At first Brandon assumed that it was his mother's age that caused her to hang back, but after only a few minutes he could tell Alexandra was trying to put some distance between the men and the women on the trail so she could have a private talk with Moira.

He was torn. He was dying to hear what kind of secrets Moira could reveal about the murder of Susan Lalo in New York. Moira also seemed to have a handle on what the friction was about between Lorna and Brian. Damn her. His mother was going digging for gossip and once again he was left to hear about it all second-hand. Well, maybe not. After all, this would be Brandon's first good opportunity to talk with Brian Epstein since Franklin's murder.

Brandon and Brian were not particularly good friends, since Brian kept mostly to himself. The two of them also seemed to know instinctively that they hadn't much in common, so any sort of relations between them were cordial, but distanced. Brandon had a similar relationship with Glenda Guilder, but that was mostly because Glenda was just too weird for words. A book on the humorous side on the history of executions? Yeesh. So knowing that his mother wanted the boys out of the way, Brandon tried to pick up his pace and stay as close to Brian as he could.

As the two of them moved rapidly over rocks and sagebrush, traveled up inclines and around scraggly creosote bushes, Brandon found himself staring at Brian's thick muscular legs. I had no idea he was in such good shape, he thought. And indeed he had always thought of the often sedentary and rather solidly built Brian Epstein to be on the soft and pudgy side. Seeing him in motion – and in walking shorts – changed his opinion quickly.

Even though it was a warm day, Brandon himself did not wear shorts. He didn't own any because his legs were so long and thin. The idea of revealing them to the world on purpose seemed out of the question. Ethan's surprisingly athletic, too. Seeing Brian's legs made Brandon remember what he thought the first time he saw Ethan Arnold working in his garden wearing gym shorts and little else.

Surprisingly athletic, he had thought. Athletic enough to … to lift 175 pounds of Franklin Crown-Smith up to the ceiling to hang him to death by his bolo tie? Perhaps not. Although it was surmised by the police that the rolling library stairs were used in some way, Brandon could not twist his brain in such a way that he could bring himself to imagine a scenario in which Ethan could have enticed Franklin to the top of those stairs and hanged him. Franklin would not have willingly climbed up the ladder with another man. Was it at gunpoint? No one in the colony owned a gun except for Moira, and that was a rifle she kept stowed secretly under her bed. It wasn't hard to imagine that Franklin might have willingly climbed the ladder with a woman. But which one and why?

"Is Lorna going to be all right?" Brandon asked Brian's hairy left calf as the calf's owner climbed up a small embankment ahead of him.

"Probably," he replied and marched on.

"You know, I've always wondered why they didn't give you just one house, since you two are a couple. You and Lorna live together in Los Angeles, don't you?"

"Uh huh. In Westwood," said Brian. "Frank and PopIris gave us a lot of problems about living together when we first applied. They said they only let one person to a house. That's it. No family members. No exceptions. We tried pointing out to Frank that technically since we weren't married, we weren't family members, but he was paranoid about anyone here sleeping together. It wasn't till we got here later I found out why."

Brian stopped talking, leaving Brandon to chew on what he just insinuated. Finally Brandon couldn't chew any more. "Why?!" he practically shouted.

"If all the women here are sleeping alone, it made it easier for Frank to have sex with them."

"You're kidding. Who?" asked Brandon before he realized all too well whom Brian was referring to. Lorna. Franklin had either slept with, or tried to sleep with Lorna Shaw. "I'm sorry," Brandon apologized. "When did you find out?"

"That bitch Glenda told me about it that night in the Penitente Room. She only told me 'cause she wanted me to get mad at Franklin, so of course I got pissed off and ... and I told him I was going to kill him if I ever caught him with Lorna again."

"I noticed you were about ready to hit him."

"Yeah," he said, and stopped and turned to face Brandon for the first time. "I didn't really mean it, you know, about killing him. I was as surprised as anybody when Ethan actually did it, but at the same time, I wasn't sorry."

"Ethan didn't kill Franklin for a couple of old photographs."

"No," Brian agreed, "he killed him because Frank found out he was growing pot in the front yard."

Was I the only one who didn't know? thought Brandon. Suddenly, he wanted to make Brian as uncomfortable as Brian was making him. "So was Glenda telling the truth? About Franklin sleeping with Lorna? I can't picture her doing something that stupid."

Brian Epstein took off his baseball cap and wiped his brow. Firmly seating his hat back on his head, he turned and started walking back again for the Box. "I don't know," he said, "I walked in on both of them one day over at Lorna's house. He had his arms around her and stuff. She was trying to get rid of him, but he wouldn't go till he saw me. Later, she told me that he tried hitting on Moira first, but she's a dyke. That only left Lorna."

"And Glenda and PopIris," added Brandon.

Brian turned and looked at him with disbelief then hooted, "In their dreams! And I bet PopIris dreamed more about him than Glenda did. That old, blind cooze has been throwing herself at Frank for twenty years now, I hear. Maybe she finally scored and he committed suicide." He laughed some more, and Brandon half-heartedly chuckled along with him just to be agreeable.

Still, the possibility of Glenda or Iris being a rejected lover and murderer had a plausible ring to it. But then again, the plausibility that Brian Epstein killed Franklin in a jealous rage seemed just as strong. And what about Moira climbing out of the skylight during the party and her connection with the murder of Susan Lalo?

It was all too much for him. "I wonder how my Mom's doing back there," he mused aloud, hoping she could be relied on again to come up with some sort of order out of all this chaos.

Thinking of his mother made Brandon realize just how far ahead of the women they had become. "I think we'd better hold up a minute, Brian. We're getting a little separated."

Brian willingly halted and parked himself on the nearest boulder. Although a cool breeze was blowing off the icy river, the rocks radiated the warmth of the sun making them feel like hard, friendly flesh to the touch. Brian opened his shirt and lay back, pulling the brim of his cap down to shade his eyes from the sun. Brandon tried hard to emulate Brian's outdoor repose, but the boulder he had chosen for himself was slightly damp and had a sharp irregularity that poked him in his left shoulder blade when he tried to lie back. After only a brief moment, he opted to once again sit precariously upright and attempt not to stare too much at Brian.

Unbuttoning his own shirt he looked down at his thin white chest and compared it with the wide strong expanse of muscle covered with black hair that was Brian's. He must lift weights, he mused, then realized that since Brian was a sculptor, his art was weight. He envisioned Brian in his workshop shirtless in front of a block of stone, hammer and chisel in hand, whacking away like a modern Michelangelo. Chances were though, Brian worked with clay, but clay wasn't nearly as fun to think about.

They chatted, the two of them, together on safe and antiseptic topics, the weather, geology, until they heard the patter of feet nearby. Alexandra and Moira emerged on the trail totally absorbed in conversation, not only did they not notice Brandon and Brian at first, but talking away, it was doubtful they noticed the entire gorge. Brian whistled to them and they sauntered over and sat next to the men.

"How are you doing, Mom?" Brandon asked as Alexandra chose a settee-sized rock upon which to sit. "Are you holding up okay?"

"Of course," she replied. "GooGoo only had to pull me up one hill ... and a half. So are we here? Is this the carton?"

"The Box," said Brian. "No, it's just up ahead. We were waiting for you to catch up."

"Whatever for? If we came to see a box, then let's see a box." Alexandra stood and dusted herself off. "Come on."

Moira looked at Brian and shrugged. Everyone got up and Brandon maneuvered next to his mother. "I'll stick with you for a while," he said. Brian and Moira started off in the lead. As their friends got sufficiently out of earshot, Brandon said conspiratorially to Alexandra, "Franklin and Lorna slept together once.

She smiled and shook her head, "No dear, Franklin and Lorna didn't sleep together once."

"But Brian walked in on them together, and ..."

"Sweetheart, Franklin and Lorna had an affair during her residency all last year."

"How did you find that out?"

"Lorna told Moira in the cab of the truck while we were driving here today."

"God. All last year?"

"Yes. And she had even been with Franklin the afternoon before the pot luck supper. The day he was killed. That's why she was running so late when we arrived."

"Does Brian know about any of this?"

Alexandra didn't answer right away. "Who knows?" she said after a thoughtful pause.

Moira and Brian were now off ahead, out of sight. Then the popping noises started. Pop-pop. Pop. Like balloons exploding at a party. The echoes of the pops reverberated throughout the canyon.

"What's that?" asked Brandon.

Alexandra, with concern spreading across her face said, "Someone is shooting a gun."

"Probably just some kids shooting at targets, right?"

Before Alexandra could speak, another pop sounded and a bullet ricocheted off a boulder not two feet from the spot she was standing. "Dear god!" she exclaimed as the two of them frantically scrambled for cover behind the nearest outcropping of stones. "Someone is target shooting all right." Another bullet struck the stone that shielded them and bounced off along with its own echo off into the gorge. "And we're it."

Brandon shushed his mother and motioned for her to try to keep her head down. Minutes passed as they both listened for danger. Above the roar of the Rio Grande it was hard to hear anything other than an occasional meadowlark, but they strained their ears at the river's white noise, and soon they realized they could definitely hear footsteps approaching.

Brandon, white-lipped and rigid in his hiding place, tried not to look over at his mother, hoping to keep their mutual fears from feeding on each other. He could hear her breathing, short little breaths that eventually stopped altogether as the footfalls grew even closer. Brandon was preparing himself mentally for all sorts of imagined confrontations, but one thing he was not prepared for was to hear a man whisper his name.

"Brandon? Brandon, are you all right?" came the insistent whispering from the voice that accompanied the footsteps.

"Brian!" he called out softly, "Brian, we're back here!"

"Where?" asked Brian Epstein's voice. Brandon kicked at a loose rock at the edge of their hiding place and waited while Brian dashed to join them in safety.

"What's happening?" asked Alexandra the minute she saw him.

"It's Moira. She's been shot."

"Oh, dear God!" wailed Alexandra.

Brandon quieted his mother and turned to Brian. "Is she alive?"

"I don't know. I'm not good at first aid and stuff. I didn't know what to do."

"I've got to get to her," said Brandon. "Where is she?"

"Close. Just around the bend. Who's doing all that shooting?"

Brandon shook his head. "I don't know. You stay here with Mom while I check on Moira."

"Brandon, no!" said Alexandra.

"I'm going for help," said Brian. "Your Mom should be safe here."

"Fine," he agreed, "but be careful."

All the blood had drained out of Brian's face. "Do you think someone's intentionally shooting at us?"

"Who cares what their intentions are, Brian?" snapped Brandon. "I think the fact that bullets are flying is reason enough. I'm going to see Moira."

"I'm coming with you," said Alexandra, suddenly composed.

"Stay here until Brian gets help."

"Certainly not. It'll take two of us to attend to Moira. Besides, we should stay together."

"Let me go first," said Brian. "It'll distract whoever that is out there and give you a clear shot."

"Rephrase that later when you think about it," she said.

Brian hesitated a brief moment then took off running back out to the truck. Before he was out of their sight, Brandon and

Alexandra leapt out from behind their rock and dashed ahead up the trail to attend to Moira. To everyone's relief, no further shots rang out.

Moira was sprawled, face down, unmoving in the middle of the trail. She had been shot twice: once through the shoulder blade and once through the back of the left leg. Brandon made his mother stand aside, sheltered in a crevice while he checked Moira for signs of life.

"She's still breathing," he announced and breathed himself for the first time in twenty minutes.

"How badly is she hurt?"

"Bad," he answered. "She's lost a lot of blood, and it looks like she hit her head when she fell." Brandon removed his shirt and started ripping it apart into large strips. He felt skinny, white and exposed but Moira's need won out over his natural modesty.

Alexandra crept cautiously back toward the two of them in the trail. "Is there anything I can do for her right now?"

"I'm trying to stop the bleeding," he said.

"Where is she wounded?"

"Here ... and here," he pointed.

"Can you tell if they entered her from the front or the back?"

Brandon looked up at his mother with puzzlement. He gently rolled Moira on her side to bandage her shoulder and studied the exit wound that emerged just under her clavicle. "From the back. Why?"

Alexandra looked around them at the canyon walls then stood with her feet to Moira's feet as she faced the direction Moira must have been standing. Once she positioned herself correctly, she turned directly around and pointed to a spot across the river, partway up the wall of the gorge. "There," she said. "That's where the gunman was. See over there where a small footpath snakes down the side of the rocks there? Someone would have been able to see all four of us from there."

"Get down!" Brandon barked at her, but she waved him away.

"There's no one there now. She's gone."

They both turned their attentions fully to the ministrations of Moira. She was still deeply unconscious and breathing only irregularly. Her heartbeat was strong though and her wounds did not seem to be mortal. After dressing her shoulder and leg as well as could be expected, they carefully moved her to a sheltered bend in the Rio Grande and washed the blood that was clotting down her back and chest with cold, clear water from the river.

"She," said Brandon once he had a moment to think.

"What was that?"

"You said 'she' before like you thought the person shooting at us was a woman."

"Yes," she said.

"Do you know who it was?" Then he stopped. "Lorna. You think it was Lorna taking pot shots at Brian, don't you?" Alexandra did not reply. "You do. You think Brian Epstein was her target and Moira just got in the way."

"Brandon ..." she began.

"But why would she try to kill him if she was the one having the affair? But yes, if Brian killed Franklin that would explain everything. She and Frank must have been really in love." Alexandra did not look at him. She simply wiped off Moira's bruised forehead with her wet scarf. "She probably followed him back the other way to the truck. Jesus! She's probably already caught up with him and killed him by now."

"No," said Alexandra, reaching over and holding him forearm, "No, I don't think it was Lorna Shaw gunning for her live-in lover."

"Then who?"

The click of a rifle's safety catch being released made them both turn their heads immediately. The arms that held the rifle were long and thin. The fingers that held the trigger were spidery and capped with short, stubby fingernails. The eye that looked through the cross-hairs was blue. The other eye was jet black glass.

"Stand up," said PopIris. "Keep your hands where I can see them."

CHAPTER THIRTEEN

"Is she dead?" asked PopIris Nelson bluntly.

"Yes," answered Alexandra before Brandon could say a word. "She died just a minute ago. We couldn't save her."

"You shouldn't have come on the hike with them, you know," Iris continued, still holding Brandon and Alexandra firmly in the eyesight of the rifle. "I didn't plan on having to kill three of you."

Having never had a loaded gun leveled at him before, Brandon marveled over the fact that he felt so calm. Must be an adrenaline rush thing, he noted to himself. Time seemed to slow and his thoughts became remarkably clear. It was probably Moira's gun she was aiming at them. Of course PopIris would have a key to Moira's house. "I didn't hear any more shots," he noted. "That means Brian got away."

"So?" intoned PopIris. "By the time he gets help to arrive, you'll be dead and I'll be long gone."

"But surely the police won't have any trouble finding you," added Alexandra.

This news did not disturb PopIris. "There's no way for them to know I did this. There's no way Epstein could have seen me."

"I told him it was you," insisted Alexandra. Brandon blanched. His mother certainly was a cool customer.

"That's a lie," said PopIris as she cocked the gun.

"No," Alexandra stated firmly, "I figured out all along that you would appear out here in the gorge somewhere. That's why I made sure Moira was never alone. What I didn't count on was that you would have a gun. I was going on the assumption that you strangled all your victims."

PopIris relaxed her aim somewhat and stared at Alexandra with a look of impressed bemusement. "Victims?" she said.

"Peggy Martinez. Sienna Sandoval. Maria Atchison. You certainly strangled all of them, and I wouldn't be surprised if there weren't others I haven't heard about, too."

"Maria Atchison?" Brandon exclaimed.

"Yes," his mother nodded, "You mentioned to me earlier that she was an opera singer. Out of curiosity, I asked Moira if her sister used a stage name and she said yes. Her sister sang under the name Susan Lalo."

Brandon still had trouble fitting the idea into his skull. "And Iris killed that girl, Sienna?"

"Yes. With her purse strap."

"Shut up!" commanded PopIris. "So it's a good thing that I got to you before you could tell anyone."

Alexandra's eyes widened. "But I have! I told it all to Detective Carson last night on the phone. He was back there, where we parked the truck. I thought up the picnic last night when we were at dinner. I knew you were about to make your move on Moira and I wanted to give you an opportunity to do it where we would be in control."

"Liar!" rasped PopIris, raising her gun at them again. Suddenly, her attention was diverted by the sounds of a helicopter rising over the rim of the canyon. Waving the barrel of her rifle at Brandon and Alexandra, she motioned for them to start walking down the trail, deeper into the canyon. "Go!" she commanded.

"Where?" asked Brandon.

"Shut up and keep moving," was her only answer. Onward then, the three of them marched, deeper into the Rio Grande Gorge, Alexandra first, followed in turn by Brandon and PopIris. The helicopter caught sight of them and followed their progress from a discrete distance. Apparently, PopIris' rifle was not difficult to spot even from long range.

She's going to hold us as hostages, thought Brandon. But where? As if in answer to his unspoken question, they rounded a final bend and saw looming up above them the specter of the Rio Grande Gorge Bridge.

The bridge above them was an architectural marvel – a single, silver arch of steel latticework supporting a two-lane road that shot across the width of the gorge rim. The bridge, completely beneath the highway, was more or less invisible from the road, giving a driver the sudden sensation of free flight. There were no cables, no towers, or overhead supports to mar the sensation that the highway levitated magically. Seen from below though, the effect was more reminiscent of the legs of the Eiffel Tower being sliced off and thrown up into the sky. Franklin had told Brandon when he first arrived that it was the highest bridge in America, meaning the distance from the road above to the canyon floor below was staggering. Looking up at it from his present angle, he did not doubt the validity of the bridge's claim to fame.

"Where are we going?" asked Alexandra.

"Follow the trail," commanded PopIris, "and keep moving."

Brandon watched his mother directly ahead of him as she picked her way cautiously over the stones of the rough-hewn trail. Every so often, she would stumble and let out a barely audible whisper of pain. He was afraid if the hike became any more difficult, Alexandra would not be able to keep up and he was uncertain just how PopIris would handle such a circumstance.

Probably cold-bloodedly, he surmised.

"Iris," he said aloud, looking hesitantly back over his shoulder at her, "let my mother go. If you need a hostage, you'll get farther and faster with just me."

"Brandon!" exclaimed his mother, stopping and turning also.

"Keep moving!" shouted PopIris. "If I have to choose between the two of you, I'll keep her."

"Oh, really?" said Brandon as he once again continued down the trail. "Why is that?"

"She's smarter and more dangerous than you are."

Well that hurt. He was in a hostage situation, exhausted, dirty, half naked, and staring death in the eye and still he felt the sting of insult and the rush of competitive jealousy over his mother's abilities. He hadn't long to brood over his lost dignity for very long before the trail started to take an abrupt upward track. He craned his neck up and followed the winding line of the path with his eyes and saw that it led six hundred fifty feet vertically, right to the bridge above them.

Alexandra, however, scoped out the ultimate destination of the trail a few seconds before he did and came to a standstill. "You've got to be joking," she gasped. "I am not going to scale any cliffs."

"Move!" shouted PopIris once more, but Alexandra stood her ground.

"No," she said plainly, "I cannot go another step further. You'll have to shoot me now."

PopIris coolly lifted up her rifle to take aim and Brandon lost all the blood out of the top half of his body. "Wait!" he shouted and pointed in the sky behind them. The police helicopter was close upon them now.

"Drop your weapons and place your hands in the air!"

Brandon obediently stared wide-eyed at the helicopter and without question raised his arms high. PopIris, on the other hand, raced past Brandon and put the muzzle of her rifle to

Alexandra's skull. "Go," she commanded and Alexandra had no choice but to continue along the trail that began to ascend sixty-five stories above them.

They had left Brandon behind. He was out of danger, but hardly relieved. No sooner had the two women rounded the first of a scary series of airborne hairpin turns, than a uniformed officer on foot was upon him. First knocking Brandon over in a blindsided tackle, he then hoisted him up quickly to his feet, forced his head down somewhere around his beltline and scurried him to what he considered to be safe haven among an outcropping of rocks.

"What are you doing?!" Brandon wailed.

"Stay down. You're safe now," roughly assured the trooper.

"Forget about me," he snapped, "stop her." He tried to wrestle his way free to get a look at his mother ascending the trail that led to the bridge at the top of the canyon, but she and PopIris were out of sight.

"Where do you think she's taking her?" Brandon asked his protector.

"The parking lot by the bridge," said the officer who was also squinting up at the trail to see if he could catch a glimpse of the fugitive women. "We got two dozen men at the bridge waiting for her to come out at the top." Brandon finally took a moment to actually look at whom he was talking with. The officer who had tackled him so brutally and dragged him off the "safety" was none other than the hulking Sergeant Cigarette from the jail house.

"Ethan!" said Brandon. "Does this mean you're going to let Ethan go?"

"Who?"

"Ethan Arnold. You've got him locked up for hanging Franklin Crown-Smith."

"He's being moved to Albuquerque for the indictment."

"But why? You're on the verge of capturing Iris Nelson any minute. Why would you go ahead and indict Ethan when you've got her?"

Sergeant Cigarette looked over at Brandon skeptically. "Are you saying that she hanged that guy?"

Brandon was about to say yes without hesitation, but hesitation crept up anyway. Indeed no one had mentioned a word about Franklin's murder today. Alexandra had pointed the finger at PopIris for strangling Moira's sister and Sienna Sandoval. PopIris had all but admitted her guilt outright. Certainly she was clearly responsible for Moira's own frightful condition, as well as the current hostage crisis. But why in the world did PopIris Nelson murder Franklin?

"Yes," said Brandon, "I think she did ... but I'm not sure." He felt so damned weak and helpless all of a sudden. Why wasn't he sure? Why didn't he even have a clue? Why was he standing down here safe when his mother was scaling a cliff with a madwoman?

Sergeant Cigarette's attention had once more wandered back to the twisting upward trail to the bridge. Alexandra and PopIris were visible once again, now about halfway up. The long muzzle of the rifle was still plainly evident and pointed in Alexandra's back.

Brandon looked around and noticed that no one was currently paying him the slightest bit of mind. He backed away silently from Sergeant Cigarette and crept unobtrusively to the trail head at the canyon floor. The uniformed personnel, having their attention diverted either to their present duties or to the women high above on the cliff, did not see Brandon until he had scaled a quarter of the way up the gorge wall.

Cigarette saw him first and gave chase. Brandon, more determined than ever to reach his mother, saw his pursuer and picked up his own pace. Shirtless, cold, scratched, bruised, and sunburned, he nevertheless found a small semblance of a second wind and kept an even distance between himself and the sergeant.

It was hard not to look down. The trail, being often used by serious hikers was not overly dangerous, but still had a difficulty level that taxed all but the heartiest of human specimens and repelled the casual picnicker. Brandon, no Olympic athlete by far, started to feel his quadriceps burn with fatigue as he scrambled up the rockier incline. It helped his climbing to muse on the thought that Brian and his thighs would probably enjoy something like this. Thinking of Brian Epstein's legs gave Brandon a bit of momentary pleasure, but his mind quickly snapped back to the terrible task at hand.

Three quarters of the way up the canyon wall, Brandon's body finally failed him. He staggered, stumbled and came to rest under a small overhang of rock that was cool and moist underneath. His heart pounded almost in sync with the rapid rise and fall of his chest as he gasped for air.

It wouldn't be long now before Cigarette caught up with him, but at that point Brandon didn't give a damn. What was he going to do, force him back down to the canyon floor? Hardly. Being most of the way to the summit, the only logical place the sergeant could possibly escort him was all the way to the top.

Brandon stood up and tried to see where his mother and PopIris had gotten to, but the trail was empty from there on. They must be at the parking lot by the bridge. He took courage in the fact he hadn't heard any more shots. But would he be able to hear them while tucked under the lip of the canyon? He didn't know. Cigarette said there were police stationed above to apprehend PopIris when she appeared, so he only hoped that she had seen no way out and surrendered quietly. He'd wait for Cigarette, then the two of them would go topside together and discover what had happened.

A scuffle of stones along the trail below foretold the imminent arrival of Sergeant Cigarette. Brandon had just about caught his breath and was readying himself to continue the climb once the sergeant got there. What he was not prepared for, though, was for the officer to appear with his weapon drawn and pointed at Brandon's face.

"Freeze!" he said.

Brandon was so taken aback that he almost burst out laughing. "What are you doing? You're going to shoot at me? For what?"

Not lowering his revolver one inch, Cigarette looked a little hesitant. "What are you trying to do?"

"My mother's in trouble. I'm just trying to get to her. Come on, let's go."

"No, we stay here out of the way until we get the all clear."

"We stay here? You've got to be joking. We're almost to the top. At least let's go up there and stay out of the way."

Sergeant Cigarette, deciding that Brandon hardly posed a serious threat to anyone at all, replaced his revolver in his holster. "Okay. Go," he said, "but before we get to the top, stop and let me go first."

"Gladly," replied Brandon who was none too keen to meet up again with PopIris's shotgun. He took one last deep breath and started up the final quarter of the path to the rim of the gorge.

When they finally approached the top, Brandon willingly stepped back and let Sergeant Cigarette pass him by. With weapon drawn, Cigarette climbed slowly and silently the final few feet in cautious preparation for what he might find at the parking lot just ahead. Brandon watched as the officer climbed the final embankment and disappeared over the top. Then silence.

He stayed behind on the trail for what was probably only three minutes, but what seemed an eternity, before curiosity got the best of him. Copying Cigarette's slow and silent approach, he completed his destination.

The parking lot at the west end of the high bridge over the Rio Grande was a rather medium-sized dirt turnout that was intended as a scenic lookout for tourists and picnickers. Tourists and picnickers, however, were not what Brandon found when he emerged from the hiking trail.

A semicircle of five police cars ringed a dark blue Saab in the center of the lot. PopIris was standing by the car with Alexandra in front of her. Iris still kept the barrel of the gun pressed firmly into Alexandra's skull, mussing her poor hostage's badly disheveled hairdo. Poor Mom, thought Brandon. He knew that by this time, Alexandra's own undignified appearance would probably be bothering her more than the threat of an untimely death. He spotted Sergeant Cigarette beside a picnic lean-to and moved stealthily to his side.

PopIris did not notice Brandon's arrival but Alexandra did. It was a fleeting moment when their eyes met. She had, as he expected, moved beyond fear at this point and had landed firmly in the realm of fatigue mixed with boredom. The look she unobtrusively shot Brandon was one of wry discomfort mixed with a little embarrassment. He had seen that look on her face twice before: once when a homeless man fell asleep on her shoulder as they rode a Philadelphia city bus; and once when he visited her moments after hemorrhoid surgery. Brandon started to smile back at her as a gesture of encouragement, but was stopped by the unexpected event of PopIris forcing Alexandra into the Saab's driver seat.

Iris climbed in the back seat and propped the gun on the driver's headrest, then the car started to pull out of the parking lot. The police not only did not try to stop them, they in fact got out of the way and let them drive by.

"What are they doing?!" shouted Brandon, which startled the nearby sergeant. "They're just going to let them drive away?!"

"Shut up," said Cigarette. "We've got this under control," and as the Saab pulled out of the lot, he left Brandon to go join the other officers in the squad cars.

PopIris's car made a hasty right and started to go across the bridge. Left alone once again, Brandon, too, scurried for the bridge to get a better view. Being on foot, he in fact made it there faster than the officers in the parking lot with their cars.

Running up on the bridge's concrete sidewalk, he soon saw why they had let PopIris try to get away. She had apparently done just what they had hoped for by making her retreat across the bridge. On the far side, New Mexico state troopers had set up an impressive roadblock of police cars and sawhorses. Approximately thirty officers were there with weapons drawn and trained on the car.

PopIris's Saab stopped dead at the center lookout point of the bridge and no one moved. Brandon looked behind to where he had come and saw that the other side of the bridge had been sealed off with police as well. He looked down and saw the Rio Grande far, far below. He looked one hundred yards ahead and saw the Saab's door open.

PopIris slowly forced Alexandra out of the car and over to the railing. She yelled at the blockade, "Let me through or she jumps!"

Brandon saw his mother glance down at the river six hundred fifty feet below then back up at PopIris. "You've got to be joking," she said, but PopIris was in no mood to be joking and was in no mood for Alexandra's dry urbanity.

Suddenly a deep voice boomed from a bull horn at the far blockade. "Alexandra, are you all right?"

"John?" said Alexandra. "Is that you? Thank god."

Detective Carson put down his bull horn and stepped forward from the group at the far end of the bridge. "Iris, put the gun down," he said, "and let's talk."

"No," she replied, "back off and let me drive out of here! And don't follow me!"

"I'm coming over."

"No!"

"Iris ...," he started, then without speaking another word, he slowly placed the bull horn on the ground. PopIris eyed him uneasily as he slowly removed his hand gun from his shoulder holster and laid it next to the horn. He removed his jacket and rolled up his sleeves, presenting himself to her with open hands as an unarmed man.

Iris was not impressed. "Stay back," she yelled and pressed the rifle a little more firmly into Alexandra's chest. Being smack up against the waist-high railing, this forced Alexandra to lean uncomfortably backwards over the chasm.

Brandon unconsciously moved forward toward the women. Pointedly ignoring Sergeant Cigarette's silent entreaties to get out of the way, he came within fifty yards of where PopIris held Alexandra. Detective Carson was another two hundred feet further off than that. As Carson slowly and calmly approached the women with soft words and open gestures, PopIris pressed the gun harder and harder into Alexandra, until at last Alexandra was showing the greatest difficulty in maintaining her balance and her grip on the rail. Iris had pushed her to the point where another inch and Alexandra would be on her way to the river.

Seeing that PopIris Nelson clearly meant business, Carson stopped advancing, but kept talking to her calmly. "Iris, let Alexandra go and we'll just talk. No one's going to hurt you. No one's going to make you do anything you don't want to do."

Brandon suddenly became aware of a subtle change in Alexandra's face. She was quickly dissolving from a facade of imperial self-control into one of ill-concealed terror. Her grip loosened. She started to tumble backwards over the rail.

Before he could even think, Brandon shouted "No!" and raced forward toward his mother. PopIris, catching sight of him for the first time, swiveled around quickly with the rifle.

With the gun pulled so rapidly away, Alexandra teetered wildly backwards over the edge of the bridge and could only save herself by kicking both her legs in wild counterbalance. Her left flailing leg found a fortunate (but unwelcome) home between PopIris' thighs. Her foot lodged firmly and painfully in her captor's pudenda.

As Alexandra made poignant contact, PopIris screamed, squeezed the trigger and fired. Brandon clearly saw the shell approach him as if in slow motion, and turning his head to escape the blast, was struck by the bullet along his left cheek bone. Falling to the ground, he did not lose consciousness, but rather had the surprising mental clarity to witness the following sequence of events while slipping slowly into shock.

Alexandra, immediately after the shot rang out, righted herself and shoved PopIris violently forward onto the pavement. Not only did the rifle go flying out of PopIris's hands, but the glass eye went flying out of PopIris' face. It bounced heinously like a child's evil toy down the double yellow line in the road before shattering into black shards.

Alexandra threw herself on top of PopIris, grabbed fistfuls of the woman's thin, black Dutch boy, and gave her hair a yank. PopIris screamed again and rolled them both over like a pair of mating turtles. Detective Carson and a dozen officers were upon them in seconds.

Freed from her captor, Alexandra stumbled quickly over to where Brandon lay on his side in the road. Sergeant Cigarette was with him already, cradling Brandon's head in his large brown hands. "Brandon!" wailed Alexandra, "Oh my god. Is he all right?"

Sergeant Cigarette inexplicably looked around at the ground where they were sprawled. Without releasing his firm grip from the side of Brandon's head, he called out, "Don't just stand there, find it!" to the officers positioned nearby. Immediately, uniformed personnel started combing the pavement in a wide circle around Brandon, Alexandra and Cigarette.

"Find what?" whispered Brandon in a voice he wasn't sure even belonged to himself.

"Oh, he's all right! Thank god!" said his mother as she brushed back the blood-clotted hair off his forehead. She looked back over her shoulder and saw Detective Carson supervise the handcuffing and arrest of PopIris Nelson. All the fight had gone out of the woman at that point. PopIris stoically allowed herself to be restrained and offered no struggle as she was advised of her Miranda rights.

To everyone's surprise, they had only just turned and started walking back to the squad cars when PopIris sprang to life once more. Kneeing one officer violently in the crotch while elbowing another in the solar plexus, she momentarily broke free from their grasp. With hands manacled at the small of her back, she ran swiftly to the nearest railing, then like some desperate, wingless bird, vaulted the rail and took flight.

The police rushed to the railing to witness her silent descent to the canyon floor. Six hundred fifty feet she plunged headfirst to the rocks below, only missing a slightly less grisly death in the Rio Grande by no more than a yard.

Alexandra and Brandon watched Iris's leap in mute astonishment. Brandon was just starting to return to his senses and was also starting to acutely feel the pain of his head wound. An EMS crew relieved Sergeant Cigarette of his viselike grip on

Brandon's head and compressed his temple with thick wads of gauze.

A cry of triumph went up from some policemen nearby. They had found the object of their quest. Cigarette walked over to the railing where the officers squatted. He shook his head, then gingerly peeled what looked like a red packing sticker off of the metal guardrail post. Dangling it from between his thumb and forefinger, he walked the object back over to the EMS crew attending Brandon. "Got it," he said and laid it in the EMS worker's outstretched hand.

Brandon curiously eyed the wrinkled red object then noticed that his mother was looking at it, too. Alexandra had started to turn a bit green when he asked her, "What's the matter, Mom? What is it?"

"It's your left ear," she said matter-of-factly.

"Oh," said Brandon with relief, "is that all?" and passed out cold.

CHAPTER FOURTEEN

Everyone got a hearty laugh once Moira finally managed to wrestle open Alexandra's gift with her one good hand. The small, old-fashioned hospital room was jammed with all the artists of the Pembroke, as well as Alexandra and Detective Carson. Brandon sat on the edge of Moira's bed and helped her clear away the wrapping paper and put the present on her head. It was a Day-Glo propeller beanie. Motorized. Brandon flipped the switch at Moira's crown and the room erupted with applause and laughter.

Moira and Brandon sitting together were quite a sight: he, with the top of his head and left ear bound up in white gauze; she, with one leg in a cast, a shoulder and arm in traction, a black and blue face, and a propeller beanie. Detective Carson took a chair near the window and asked, "How's your head, Brandon?"

"Fine," he said. "They reattached everything okay. Only I have this weird urge to go out and paint sunflowers." Moira socked him in the arm and they both yelled ow together.

Ethan stood quietly by the door beside P.J. Copeland. He stared serenely at Brandon with his arms folded over his chest. P.J. fidgeted nervously, not knowing quite what to do with himself in such a circumstance. Lorna and Brian embraced in a corner, and Glenda Guilder inspected the uneaten food on Moira's tray.

"Thank God this is all over," said Brandon to Carson.

"It's not quite," he replied. "'Fraid that's why I'm here."

"I thought you came to see me," said Moira petulantly.

Alexandra looked first to Detective Carson, then over to Moira. "Well ... yes, dear. We did. But there still are one or two more little matters John needs to attend to."

"What's that?" asked Brian.

Glenda Guilder looked up and hypothesized, "We have to find out if the Pembroke still exists and if they're going to keep us here."

"No ... not that," Alexandra said with reluctance.

"I still have an arrest to make for Franklin Crown-Smith's murder," said Carson. Everyone but Alexandra looked startled.

"I don't understand," said Brandon looking worriedly over at Ethan. "When? Who?"

"Right here and now," the detective said, standing up. "I've got men right outside the door."

Brian scowled. "What about Iris?" he said. "You mean to tell me you don't think she did it?"

Alexandra and Carson looked at each other. He nodded to her as permission to explain. "No," she said, "Iris came gunning for us in the canyon because she figured out Moira killed Franklin."

"What?!" said Brandon so loudly he hurt his stitches. Moira looked surprised at this news and did not reply at all.

"Oh, Iris was a smart cookie," Alexandra continued. "She wasn't kidding when she said Franklin owed all his success to her, because it was probably true. She was completely, hopelessly devoted to him. Iris was with Franklin for ... what did she say at dinner that night, Brandon? Fourteen years? Well, she was lying. She'd been with him from the day she was born. When we were in Farmington, Franklin's mother showed me a picture of him as a teenager surrounded by his girlfriend, Peggy Martinez, and three of Matilda Chimoro's daughters. One of them looked familiar, but I didn't make the connection until Iris said she moved to New York in 1983. That was the same year Franklin moved to New York. She also said she was married briefly, apparently to some man named Nelson, so that was why she didn't use the name Chimoro any longer.

"Once I realized that Iris had been with Franklin for a lifetime, the rest was easy. Every time he had a serious relationship, the woman he loved was murdered. If Franklin, being left-handed, couldn't have killed those girls, then Iris, being right-handed, could."

Detective Carson took out a small notepad shook his head in amazement. "Peggy Martinez in Farmington, Susan Lalo in New York, Sienna Sandoval here in Taos. One, two, three … right down the line."

"But what does that have to do with Moira?" asked Glenda.

"Susan Lalo," answered Carson, closing his notepad. "Stage name used by Maria Atchison."

"She was my sister. We used to live together in New York," said Moira quietly.

"Oh."

Carson stood up and put his hands in his pockets. "I got a copy of the old report from the Manhattan D.A. Moira Atchison came home one night and found her sister murdered. Right after that, Franklin Crown-Smith, her fiancé, was arrested, briefly detained, and released."

"The police told me my sister had walked in on a burglar, who killed her," said Moira. "I never believed that for a minute. I always knew who did it. And now you're saying it wasn't Frank at all? You're saying it was PopIris?"

"Appears so," confirmed the Detective. "According to the reports, Lalo's killer was tall, right-handed, and had short nails. That seems to fit Iris Nelson fairly well."

Alexandra laid her hand on Moira's leg cast. "The problem was Iris knew you suspected Frank, too. I'm afraid you made a grave mistake when you used your sister's photo to apply for your residency here."

"That was your sister's photo?" said Brandon before he realized that it was not common knowledge that he and his mother had snooped in everyone's personal file. "I mean ... why did you send Maria's picture instead of your own?"

"To be mean," she said. "I wanted to make Frank sweat."

Alexandra gave an ironic nod, "Of course then somebody killed Franklin and Iris went nuts – once she was certain who was to blame."

"Me," said Moira flatly.

Alexandra continued, "Well, she thought it was you all along because of that picture you sent of your sister. She suspected you were gunning for Franklin – or something like that. Probably, she accepted you to the colony so she could strangle you, too – but then Frank had to go have an affair with Sienna Sandoval. Planning that murder must have diverted her attention from you until Frank ended up getting killed. Actually, she wasn't certain you were the one who killed him till I stupidly put a new idea into her head. That was completely all my fault."

"What are you talking about, Mom? You mean, that stuff we said about P.J. that night PopIris took us to dinner?"

"Huh?" grunted the startled boy.

Alexandra turned and gestured grandly toward P.J. Copeland. "That boy," she proclaimed, "is definitely some sort of genius. You just don't know." P.J. looked as confused as anyone. Alexandra went on. "The poem. The poem he made up the night of the pot luck was really the key to everything." P.J. looked very confused and uncomfortable with the amount of attention he was suddenly getting. Alexandra's attention in particular made him even more nervous. "Why were you late for the party that night?" she inquired.

Ethan put his arm around the boy's shoulder and asked, "Why? What does it matter?"

"It matters a great deal," she said. "Why don't I tell you what I suspect and you can tell me if I'm wrong. All right?" P.J. and Ethan exchanged looks. "Well, I imagine that you walked by Lorna's house a couple of hours before you got there, went somewhere else, then came back to the party. During that time, you saw something important and then made up a poem about it later. How am I doing?"

P.J. looked at Ethan, then back at Alexandra. He didn't say anything. Alexandra continued.

"When I realized this, I was at dinner with Brandon and Iris. And I spilled all the beans in front of the very person I shouldn't have."

"But what you said was absurd," argued Brandon. "You thought it was possible that while Moira was washing the stage blood off in the bath, P.J. saw her climb out of the skylight and go to Franklin's house."

"It's not absurd at all. And anyway, it must have made sense to Iris. Thanks to her informer, little Miss Glenda here, she'd narrowed the field down to Brian, Ethan, and Moira. And since she knew Moira was dangerous to begin with, well what I said must have tipped her scales."

Moira was still chewing on what Brandon had just said. "I climbed out of the what?"

"Out of the skylight, dearest. I suggested to Iris that you had pre-recorded bathing sounds on the tape recorder you took into the bathroom with you. You had a good half hour to climb out of the skylight, lure Franklin up on the library stairs and hang him, climb back in the bathroom and re-emerge at the party, and none of us would think you were gone. I told Iris, however, that

P.J. must've seen you, and put the image of you rising through the roof into his poem."

"But I didn't!" protested Moira. "I was really in the bathtub that whole time!"

"Well, yes I realize that now because of two things. First of all, I snuck into your house today – sorry – and I listened to the other side of the tape you played at the party. It was Gershwin, not bathing sounds. Secondly, I realized that P.J. was standing there during your whole performance. He must have seen someone else climbing out of the roof earlier that evening. P.J. couldn't have seen you do anything while you were in the tub because he was in the room with us."

Moira was obviously relieved to hear this, but P.J. started biting his lower lip and tapping his left foot. All attention turned to Ethan and P.J. at that point. Detective Carson walked over to them and stood in front of the boy.

"Did you see someone climbing out of the roof that night, son?" he said. P.J. nodded a little. "Who was it?" P.J. shrugged.

Alexandra said to P.J., "It's all right to tell us, we already know. There was only one possibility."

"There was?" said Brandon.

"Well, think back," she said. "Moira was not the only one to take a bath that night. Who did you see, P.J.? You can tell us."

P.J. hesitated, then pointed slowly to Lorna Shaw.

Brian Epstein looked down at her and released his hold. Tears began to well up in her eyes as she saw Detective Carson walk toward her. She moved away from his advance and pressed her back up against the window sill. "It was an accident," she said. "I didn't mean … I didn't know."

"You had an affair with him," Alexandra said.

"No! It's not what you think! That was all over. We were collaborating on my opera. No one was supposed to know he was the one who was writing the lyrics. He was working under a pen name. He wanted the whole thing to be a secret."

Glenda Guilder was taken aback. "Franklin was the Indian woman who wrote those short stories? My God."

"Yes," said Lorna. "I was working with him all afternoon. That's why I wasn't ready for that damned pot luck."

"You killed him?" said Brian with disbelief. "You really killed Franklin?"

"No," she said quickly. Then, like a true penitent, her story came rushing from her headlong. "We had an affair last year, but it was all over. That's why I wanted Brian here with me this time. After Sienna went away, Frank started getting all drunk and horny and was pressuring me to start having sex with him again. So we had a big fight and … It was so stupid, but … I left, and went back to my house. I realized my music score was with him over at the Casa. You know, I needed it for later, to play at the pot luck, and I had to get it back and I didn't want Brian to know where I left it. Glenda told him about the affair we had – and a couple days before that, he caught Frank making advances on me. Brian was just so pissed at both of us, I didn't want him to know Franklin and I were working together. I told Brian I was in Santa Fe that afternoon before the dinner."

"So you climbed out the skylight of your bathroom right after we got to the party," said Alexandra.

"Yes. I'd done it before. Brian had a habit of watching my front door. Anyway … I went back over to see Frank. He'd been drinking and was in this vile mood. He'd just found out about the pot luck we were having and was so pissed. He started getting all paranoid about how everybody was conspiring behind his back and saying how it was against all the colony rules and stuff. What he was really upset about was that I wouldn't sleep with him anymore. So I just told him I wanted my score back, and he said he had stuck it up on the top shelf of the library where nobody would find it.

"We went into the Penitente Room and I climbed up to the top of those rolling stairs to get it. He climbed up there behind me. At first it seemed like kind of a joke thing, you know, he was looking up my shirt from below and feeling up my leg. He then climbed up higher and started hugging me from behind and kissing me on the neck and then ..." Lorna stopped.

"And then what?" asked Carson.

"Then he started laughing at me. He said he didn't know why he was giving me back that music because our collaboration was over. He got the piece considered at the Santa Fe Opera, but they found my music too ... boring. They wanted his book with someone else's score. So he laughed at me and told me maybe I could sleep my way back to the top. I got mad and I slapped him. He slapped me back and nearly knocked me off the ladder. He caught me from falling and pulled me close and I started to pull away from him, but he kissed me. Hard. It was a mean kiss, it was really hard and spiteful and I struggled to get away from him, but the more I struggled, the more he liked it. I was getting really scared, too, being up on top of those wobbly stairs. Anyway, so I was struggling and I grabbed him by his bolo tie to pull him away ... and then I saw the hook right near us."

She stopped and took a breath.

"I looped his tie on the hook ... and I jumped."

Everyone in the room was perfectly silent.

"I didn't mean to do anything. I just wanted to get him away from me. I fell to the ground and just grabbed my score and ran out of the room as fast as I could. I didn't even look back. I thought he'd be caught there at the top of the stairs and wouldn't be able to get down to me. I had no idea he was dead. Until the next morning."

Lorna looked so sad and frightened Brandon's heart broke for her. "So you're going to charge her with murder?" he asked Detective Carson. "It sounds like an accident or self defense. Do you have to arrest her right now?"

"We'll have to take her in," he replied. "There'll be an investigation, of course. If we find it was accidental or self-defense, that'll be it. She's going to have a bit of company in the meantime, though."

"Like who?" wondered Brian.

"We need one question answered right away, Miss Shaw," said Detective Carson. Lorna looked at him apprehensively. He turned away from her and asked, "Did you notice anything unusual about the Penitente Room when you went in there with Franklin that night? Was it dark outside?"

"No," said Lorna. "It was right before sunset. Why?"

"Were the windows open or shut?"

"They were ... closed. It was getting chilly. We remarked on it at the time."

"And was anything missing from the room?"

Lorna thought long and hard about this, then shook her head. "No, I didn't notice anything different about the room."

"What he wants to know is," clarified Alexandra before Carson could speak again, "were the Ansel Adams photos on the wall?"

"Yeah. Of course they were," she said. "One was crooked and Franklin straightened it."

Detective Carson moved easily to the door. "That's what we needed to know," he said, opening the door wide. Officers Campbell and Cigarette appeared. They blocked the entryway. Carson then went over and stood in front of P.J. and Ethan. "Ethan Arnold, Peter James Copeland, you are under arrest on suspicion of burglary and suspicion of conspiracy to commit burglary."

Brandon stood up and opened his mouth to say something, but his mother grabbed him by the hand and shook her head to quiet him. He could only stand there, mute, as Ethan and P.J. were read their rights and escorted out of the room by the two uniformed officers.

Carson gently extended his hand toward Lorna and looked at her reassuringly. She looked to Brian Epstein for some sort of help or guidance, but Brian could offer her none. Turning from her lover, she took the detective's hand and allowed him to escort her from the room.

Brandon and Brian started to follow them, but Alexandra held her son back. "Let them go," she said. Brian went out of the room, leaving Glenda and Moira, Alexandra and Brandon alone.

Glenda, losing interest rapidly in the day's events, began to gather her belongings. "I suppose that's it for the Pembroke then, wouldn't ya say? I turned down two residencies at Yadow and the Zen Mountain Monastery to come here. And grant money, too. Maybe I should apply for Franklin's job. What do you think?" The three by the bed just looked at her. Glenda grinned and shrugged and left the room.

Brandon sat silently and stared at the door, remembering how Ethan looked a moment ago under the harsh hospital lights as the police led him away. Remembering how Ethan looked under the strobe of police lights the first time Brandon saw him arrested. Remembering how he looked, shirtless, in the harsh afternoon sunlight that day at the pueblo.

Alexandra and Moira sat and watched Brandon as he stared intently at the door. Moira reached up with her good hand and took the propeller beanie off her head. She then stroked him gently on the back of his shoulder and said, "I'm sorry about Ethan."

Brandon snapped out of his reverie. Were his thoughts and feelings that transparent? Did his mother notice him mooning over Ethan, too? A jolt of the tired habit of apprehension quickly shot through him, but surprisingly, he let it go. He just didn't care anymore if his mother knew about his feelings toward men or not.

"Thanks," he said to Moira. Alexandra sat still and did not say a word.

CHAPTER FIFTEEN

As they walked out the front door of the hospital, a breeze caught Alexandra's hair. Several long locks escaped their bondage and flapped playfully across her nose. She handed Brandon her purse and quickly started emergency reconstruction. The two of them stood stock still, right in the electric eye of the automatic door, as Alexandra pulled and placed bobby pins in and out of her head like an old-time telephone operator patching through connections. The door slid open and banged shut seven times before they were ready to proceed.

Brandon hated it when she made him hold her purse. He was well aware that his discomfort with the purse was just his discomfort with his own masculinity (or lack thereof), nevertheless he still found it embarrassing to hold a woman's purse in public. As he stood there with the handbag trying to look nonchalant, he wondered how much his mother actually knew about the unspoken things he felt. Could she see, as Moira could, that he was in love with Ethan? It was the first time he had ever actually admitted himself that he was in love. The prospect was so wonderful and awful at the same time, he wished he could at least mention something about it to his mother, but he couldn't. Not now. Now he would just hand her back her purse and they would walk on.

"So what are you going to do now?" he asked her as they continued out to the parking lot and her rental car.

"My flight's in about five hours," she said looking at her watch. "It's a two hour drive, so I thought I'd head on out in case I wanted to shop along the way. I can't believe I completely missed Santa Fe! I'll have to come back, there's just no two ways about it. How long will you be staying here?"

"I don't know. I was supposed to be here another month, but now we don't know if there's any 'here' here." He hoped, silently, that he could stay long enough to see Ethan's latest troubles through, and then he'd figure out the rest of his life from there. But Ethan was back in jail and Alexandra could have prevented it, but did not. "Mother," he said sternly, "why didn't you say anything when they arrested Ethan again? How could you just sit there and let them take him away?"

Alexandra reached her car and fumbled through her purse for her keys. She did not look at Brandon as she said, "Because we were wrong. He actually did steal those photos the night Franklin was killed."

"How can you say that?"

Alexandra unlocked her door and opened it. A whiff of hot air drifted out from the car's interior, so she rolled down the drivers' window and stood by the open door to let the inside cool. "Because it doesn't add up any other way. If Iris had done it to frame Ethan for Franklin's murder, she would've had to plant those photos in Ethan's house before she even found out that Franklin was dead. Now that doesn't make much sense. Couple it with the fact that Ethan was predisposed to steal Ansel Adams photographs, Ethan left the party early, Ethan's boot prints were right outside the window, and Ethan had possession of the photos, it would seem to indicate that Ethan is probably guilty."

"But you didn't think so before!" asserted Brandon, flying in the face of all reason.

"What threw me off was the fact I didn't think anyone would want those photographs badly enough to kill for them," she said. "Ethan is a very nice person, clearly not a murderer, but still the man does have a problem when it comes to Ansel Adams. I don't know how he convinced P.J. to try and steal the pictures first, but thank God the poor boy lost his nerve. What's really unfortunate is that the room was so dark as Ethan came through the window, he didn't see Franklin hanging from the ceiling. Had he noticed Franklin, I hazard to guess that Ethan would have left the photographs alone."

Probably true, thought Brandon. Poor Ethan. Hiding the photos badly behind the couch, and concocting the story about Franklin placing them there, was apparently all that he had time to do before the police burst in to search. Seducing P.J. into stealing the pictures for him was another matter. Brandon felt jealous. Jealous and betrayed.

Alexandra climbed into the car and shut the door. "It's going to be good to go home and stay home for awhile," she said through the open window.

"What about the film festival in Madagascar?"

"Oh, that," she said without batting an eye. "That's not for months and months. I have to take care of matters in North Carolina first. I'm sure the Tobacco Sheik will want to reconcile, but I don't know. And who knows whom I'll meet after the divorce comes through. Believe me, before I head down the aisle of a church the next time, I'm hiring a private detective first. Anyway, I'm off."

Alexandra made Brandon bend down to her so she could give him a kiss on the cheek. She started up the car and put it in reverse. "By Mom," he said.

She put on her sunglasses. "And Brandon," she added casually, "as long as you've decided not to date women, at least try not date any more criminals. My life is full enough."

Alexandra backed her car out of the parking space and sped off, leaving Brandon dumfounded in the lot.

He felt a giddy mixture of relief and sadness as he watched her car head down the road for Albuquerque. He turned and started walking back to his studio at the Pembroke. So Ethan really was a thief, and Alexandra really wasn't blind. Having been both in and out of love in the last ten minutes, Brandon couldn't decide just how or what he felt about anything. I should be alone for awhile, he thought.

He stopped. What is at the Pembroke for him now? Nothing. There was nothing for him at home in Philadelphia, either. He turned around and walked the other way. The Taos County Courthouse was only a few blocks off.

No, he realized, he shouldn't be alone. He should be with Ethan.

ABOUT THE AUTHOR

Toronto journalist **J. Timothy Hunt** is a regular contributor to many of Canada's most prominent magazines. He is the recipient of four National Magazine awards and two prestigious Canada Council Creative Writing Grants.

During his 16 years as a resident of New York City, he became known as a playwright and author of science fiction short stories. His plays *Angel Fire* and *The Lunatic* were presented Off-Off Broadway. His short fiction can be found in the anthologies *Lovers and Other Monsters* and *Don't Open This Book*, both published by Doubleday. He has been writer in residence three times at the Helene Wurlitzer Foundation of New Mexico, and was the founder of The Writers' Workout creative writing studio in New York. He received a B.A.A. in Journalism from Toronto's Ryerson University in 1999.

Hunt has written for many publications in Canada, including *National Post Business*, *Toronto Life*, *Elm Street*, *Reader's Digest*, and *Saturday Night*. A feature article in *Saturday Night* in June 2000 about Owens Wiwa, brother of controversially-executed Nigerian environmentalist Ken Saro-Wiwa, was expanded in 2005 into a book about the ordeal, *The Politics of Bones*.

Hunt was born and raised in Los Angeles, California. He became a Canadian citizen in 2004, and resides in Toronto, Canada, with his husband and twin sons.